THE BEST MAN

Journalist Elinor Dale is heartbroken when she is jilted by her fiancé, Jean Pierre Pascal. Seeking an explanation for his behaviour from his elder brother Luc, Elinor concludes that Luc had blocked the marriage because he suspected she was marrying into his wealthy family for monetary gain. She hoped never to see Luc again, but when their paths later cross in France, an attraction flares between them. However, Elinor finds her past love for Jean Pierre still holds her captive . . .

Books by Janet Cookson
in the Linford Romance Library:

QUEST OF THE HEART
MASQUERADE
TO LOVE FOR EVER
THE FAITHFUL HEART
A LOVE RECLAIMED
SPANISH TRYST

JANET COOKSON

✕ THE BEST MAN

Complete and Unabridged

LINFORD
Leicester

First published in Great Britain in 2001

First Linford Edition
published 2002

British Library CIP Data

Cookson, Janet
  The best man.—Large print ed.—
Linford romance library
  1. Love stories
  2. Large type books
  I. Title
  823.9'14 [F]

ISBN 0–7089–9925–5

Published by
F. A. Thorpe (Publishing)
Anstey, Leicestershire

Set by Words & Graphics Ltd.
Anstey, Leicestershire

Printed and bound in Great Britain by
T. J. International Ltd., Padstow, Cornwall

This book is printed on acid-free paper

1

As the vintage Rolls Royce travelled along the winding country lanes at a sedate pace Elinor gazed out on the sunlit hedgerows, laden with hawthorn blossom, and decided it was a perfect day for a wedding, especially her own. Her father echoed her sentiments.

'The sun is shining just for us, Ellie. For once Jean Pierre won't be able to tease us about our weather.'

Elinor smiled.

'True, and as I asked the caterers to provide only French cuisine at the reception I know he'll be delighted with the food, too!'

As they laughed together Elinor sank back into the soft, leather upholstery and marvelled at how calm and relaxed she felt on what was, after all, the most momentous day of her life. No doubt her serenity was due to the fact that, after weeks of effort, she had the satisfaction of knowing that everything had been planned down to the tiniest detail.

'You know, Dad, with our work commitments, Jean Pierre and I would never have been able to hope for such an elaborate wedding without you here, shouldering most of the burden. We owe it all to you.'

'I was delighted to help. You're my only child, Ellie, and I wanted today to be very special, to be treasured for ever. It's, well, it's what your mother would have wanted.'

She reached across to squeeze his hand in a wordless gesture of sympathy, not trusting herself to speak. The sudden loss of her mother, two years before, had shaken her to the core and Elinor knew she would always regret the fact that she had died before witnessing her blossoming career as a foreign correspondent. After such a blow, her father had struggled to re-establish his life but he had, generously, encouraged her to pursue a career which would take her abroad and which, now, was to take her as a bride to another country.

The car drew to a halt outside the wrought iron archway interwoven with wild roses which led to the parish church of St Michael's and as James Dale handed his daughter out of the car, she was surrounded by a group of well-wishers. Allowing himself a moment of fatherly pride he watched her graciously accepting the congratulations of friends and neighbours and decided he had never seen a more beautiful bride.

Her dark hair had been drawn back from her face into an elegant chignon, the austere style highlighting her delicate bone structure, wide expressive mouth and, most noticeably of all, the startling darkness of her eyes. The oyster silk column dress, hand-embroidered with seed pearls, showed off her tall, slender figure to perfection and, not for the first time, James wished that its designer, and Elinor's best friend, Catriona, had been able to join them today and fulfil her intended rôle as Elinor's bridesmaid. But, when a dream assignment had arisen for Catriona to work with a major dress designer in Paris, Elinor had, unselfishly, insisted that she put her career first.

She had no need of a bridesmaid, she had declared. The presence of her father was all she needed on her special day, and, although James knew it was a blow to lose Catriona, he hoped with all his heart that he had risen to the occasion and provided her with all the love and support she so richly deserved. From the corner of his eye he could see the figure of the vicar pacing up and down outside the church door and a glance at his watch prompted him to touch his daughter on her arm.

'Darling, we're rather late and I've just caught a glimpse of the vicar's face. He's looking rather anxious.'

Elinor broke away from her friends

with a smiling farewell and hooked her arm through her father's.

'Let's not keep the guests waiting any longer then.'

Although kindly, the vicar was inclined to be highly strung and his air was decidedly distracted as he greeted them.

'You look lovely, Elinor. Your mother would have been so proud.'

His voice lowered almost to a whisper.

'The thing is, my dear, neither the groom nor the best man has arrived yet and as we are already running rather late, I wondered if you knew of any reason for their absence.'

As her father's hand tightened protectively on her arm Elinor tried to answer the vicar's query.

'I don't understand why they're not here. Jean Pierre and his brother, Luc, are only staying at the Red Lion in the village. They really should be here by now.'

Her voice trailed away as a shiver

went through her and her father and the vicar began to talk, rapidly, in unison. The vicar went back inside.

'He's going to have the organist play some hymns for the congregation until Jean Pierre arrives,' Elinor's father said.

Elinor nodded absentmindedly. Rapt in her own thoughts it was a moment or two before the sound of an approaching vehicle registered and then her face lit up as a car screeched to a halt nearby. They were here!

She whipped round but when a tall figure stooped beneath the archway and then straightened, the smile of greeting froze on her face. Luc Pascal was alone and, dressed in a black T-shirt and denims, it was quite clear that he was not going to preside as a best man today. A few strides of his long legs brought them face to face. Elinor felt as though someone else was speaking for her when she voiced her worst fear.

'Jean Pierre isn't coming, is he?'

Luc inclined his dark head.

'I am afraid not, Elinor.'

Although it was the answer she was expecting each word seemed to tear into her and, in spite of the heat of the day, she felt cold streaming into her bones as she waited for him to continue. He drew a deep breath.

'He told me late last night that he could not go through with the wedding, but he did promise to speak with you himself. Unfortunately, this morning I found that he had gone. I knew he must have taken a cab to the nearest railway station so I went after him. I wanted to persuade him to tell you of his decision to your face, but I was too late, Elinor. He had already caught the train to London. I am so very sorry.'

Elinor could sense the shock emanating from her father's rigid figure but, although she shared his sense of betrayal and anger, only one thought was uppermost in her mind.

'Why? Why has he done this to me when only yesterday he promised to love me for ever?'

Luc Pascal's face tightened fractionally.

'He left a note for you, Elinor.'

The parchment-coloured writing paper, embossed with Jean Pierre's name and Parisian address in the right-hand corner, was familiar from countless love letters but, as Elinor took in the flowing script, the hot sting of tears almost obscuring her vision, she could barely take in the fact that she was reading something which spelled the ruin of all her dreams. It was short and to the point:

Elinor, chère,

I will always love you. But, for your sake, I cannot marry you. Please do not be angry with me. I would have done anything to avoid hurting you but circumstances beyond my control have forced me to abandon our wedding. I will keep you in my heart for ever.

Jean Pierre.

'This tells me nothing,' she whispered in disbelief.

She scrunched up the note and held

it in one clenched fist as her father looked on, his face ashen. As misery threatened to engulf her she struggled for inner control, reminding herself that her first priority had to be the family and friends who had come to witness a union that was not to be.

'You poor darling. I'll take you home straight away,' her father began but she rounded on him.

'No, Dad, I need you here. The guests need to be told what has happened. Would you do that for me?'

'Of course, Ellie, but what about you? I can't leave you alone.'

'I will escort Elinor home.'

Surprised eyes turned on Luc Pascal. They had almost forgotten the presence of the tall Frenchman who had stood aside as they contemplated their dilemma. As her father flashed her an anxious, enquiring glance Elinor made up her mind.

'That would seem to be the best solution. Thank you, Luc.'

As she took the arm that he offered

she handed over her bouquet of early summer flowers to her father.

'The vicar will be able to use these in the church. As for the reception, please take all the guests there, Dad. There's no need to waste all the delicious food that's been prepared just because the . . . because we . . . '

Her voice broke on a sob but just as her father reached out to her she turned a resolute back and set off down the path.

No one will see me cry today, she vowed. I will do my weeping in private.

The driver of the Rolls Royce fixed her with a curious stare as they passed by but she averted her eyes, her head high, as Luc led her to his car, a bronze, open-topped sports model which he had hired for his stay in England. Thankfully, the group of well-wishers had melted away but Elinor knew she and Luc would be the object of scrutiny as they drove through the village. She was grateful when, without asking, he placed a lightweight summer jacket around her shoulders, enabling her to feel far less conspicuous.

Elinor remembered little of the return journey, her eyes fixed ahead, unseeing, her mind in turmoil, and when they arrived back at Fairhaven, her family home, she knew she was close to breaking point and wanted only to go to her room and give vent to her feelings.

She said as much to Luc as she unlocked the front door but he sounded as though he would brook no refusal when he replied, 'I will stay a little while, Elinor. I feel I owe you that.'

'Please yourself,' the muffled reply came as she headed for the stairs.

Once inside her room she leaned against the closed door, hot tears scalding her cheeks as she gave way at last to the pain coursing through her. Unsought, the image of Jean Pierre's handsome, smiling face, hazel eyes twinkling at some shared joke, flashed before her and she squeezed her eyes shut in an effort to expel him from her mind, as she must now expel him from her life.

Why, her mind shrieked once more. Why had he treated her with such brutal contempt when, during the time of their whirlwind romance, he had made her feel as though she was the most desirable woman in the world? His love had helped her to emerge from the shadow cast by her mother's death and made her feel truly alive again. Had it all been a sham? Had she allowed herself to be duped? She didn't know and, the storm of weeping over, she covered her face with her hands and remained motionless, too drained to think of what to do next.

She threw off her satin shoes and then, filled with a frantic need to take off her wedding dress, she found herself frustrated by the fact that the pearl buttons which ran down the bodice had to be unfastened one by one. Haste made her clumsy but, at last, she was able to slide the gown on to her hips and then step out of it.

Relief swept over her as she left the discarded garment in a crumpled heap on the floor and walked over to her dressing-table. When she had last looked into this mirror happiness had added an expectant colour to her cheeks and a sparkle to her blue eyes. Now a pale, wide-eyed stranger stared back at her. She gave her head a sudden shake and set about removing the silk orchid which held her hair in place. A moment later she was able to loosen her hair and, after shaking it into a dark cloud, felt satisfied that every vestige of her bridal wear had now been removed.

Slipping on her robe she wandered across to the window, pushed it wide open and breathed in the heavy air scented by the lilac which rested against the wall below. Her room overlooked the back of the house and it was a view she had loved all her life. She was feeling much calmer, unnaturally so, in fact, and her mind began to pick once more over the events of her humiliation.

Had Jean Pierre simply got cold feet?

There was no doubt that when she had first met him, during her time spent on an assignment in Paris, he had been enjoying the full fruits of a bachelor life. With his boyish good looks and personable manner he was always a hit at the parties attended by the Press pack but it hadn't been long before he had begun to single out Elinor. Then, everything seemed to blur for her as the attraction that had flared between them deepened and within weeks, to her delight, he had proposed. Had he been regretting his rashness ever since and been looking for a way out?

She focused her mind on the last two weeks since they had been in England to make the final preparations for their wedding. Try as she might she could detect no change in his manner. But there had been something. When Luc had arrived a week ago, Jean Pierre had seemed a little nervous about introducing them for the first time. She had put this down to the fact that, naturally, Jean Pierre would want his brother's approval, especially as the Pascals were an old French family with traditional attitudes.

In the event, the meeting had passed off well enough, although Elinor had found Luc very different from her fiancé. His manner was reserved, austere even, well-suited no doubt to the position he held as head of the family business, but a little forbidding in a future brother-in-law. Elinor was surprised, too, at the difference in their appearance. Luc's tall, lean physique was in sharp contrast to Jean Pierre's wiry build and his raven-coloured hair and deep-set dark eyes made him look far more exotic than his fairer, younger brother.

In spite of Luc's rather flamboyant looks, though, their subsequent meetings confirmed the impression of a man who held his own counsel although, on occasion, Elinor surprised a covert look in her direction, convincing her that she was the object of scrutiny. Had that assessment found her wanting? Had she been deemed unsuitable to join one of the oldest families in France, and was the concern Luc Pascal had displayed on her behalf genuine or false? There was only one way to find out. She must confront him. She went into her bathroom, washed away the evidence of her tear-streaked face, took a deep, steadying breath and then set off for the drawing-room.

Luc was at the open french windows and turned at her approach, his eyes taking in the full-length robe in raw burgundy silk, the tumbling disarray of her hair and a face so pale that her skin seemed almost translucent. In the uncomfortable silence that followed Elinor drew moistened palms down the smooth material of her robe and wondered for just how long he was going to stand and stare at her with that dark, unfathomable expression!

As though hastily recalling his social skills he motioned towards an armchair and said, 'Elinor, please, sit down. I will make you some coffee.'

'No, nothing to drink, just some answers, please.'

His shoulders rose in a resigned shrug.

'Of course, whatever you wish, but you are looking so very pale I think we should both sit down.'

A good suggestion, Elinor decided, as she chose a small leather couch. Luc might be a little less intimidating if they were on the same level! As he took a few steps towards her Elinor thought, for one awful moment, that he was going to join her on the couch but he turned aside and settled himself into a nearby armchair.

'Luc,' Elinor began cautiously, 'you must know more than you admitted this morning about Jean Pierre's decision to leave me at the altar. You're his brother. He must have confided in you.'

'Elinor, he told me only what he wrote in that letter to you. He insisted that, for your sake, he could not marry you. That is all I know.'

She felt sure he knew more and was just playing with words:

'And you didn't press him for a fuller explanation?'

Incredulity etched every word but he met her accusing eyes with a glance as unyielding as his reply.

'I did not consider it right to pry into Jean Pierre's deepest feelings. That was between you and him and, as I explained earlier, I was expecting him to speak with you himself. Unfortunately that did not happen.'

That was another unexplained mystery! Luc was now coolly surveying the backs of his hands and Elinor felt a perverse desire to pierce the armour of this self-possessed man who seemed to be showing scant regard for the devastation his brother had caused. She cleared her throat and tried another tack.

'You know, Jean Pierre seemed a little nervous before you and I met for the first time. After all, you are his elder brother and head of the family. Had you expressed doubts to him about our engagement?'

Something like consternation fleeted across his face and Elinor was aware, for the first time, that she had hit a raw nerve.

'I admit I was a little shocked by the speed of my brother's decision. The Pascal family is, unfortunately, still rooted in the past. Although Father is dead and Mother lives abroad there is an extended family of aunts, uncles and cousins who love to run our lives for us. They, too, were a little taken aback by Jean Pierre's recklessness and I did pass these concerns on to my brother.'

Recklessness! With the choice of that one word to describe the love affair between herself and Jean Pierre he had revealed the utter contempt he held her in. Making no attempt to mask her anger she snapped.

'In other words I was not considered good enough to join the Pascal family. Not rich enough, not influential enough, and, what's more, from another country!'

'No! Elinor, you twist my words!'

He was leaning forward, dark, intent eyes fixed on hers.

'When I met you I realised you were not the . . . not a . . . '

'Gold-digger!' Elinor completed for him, her eyes blazing. 'You thought I was after nothing more than Jean Pierre's money?'

Without waiting for a reply she rose, contempt evident on her face as she looked down at him.

'It's no wonder Jean Pierre abandoned our wedding after listening to this poison. For your information the thought of money never entered my head. I loved Jean Pierre for himself but, clearly, that is not good enough in the mercenary world you inhabit. Goodbye, monsieur, I don't expect we will meet again.'

As she fled from the room she heard him call out her name but closed her ears, determined to block any attempts at a friendly approach.

★ ★ ★

'I posted my engagement ring to Jean Pierre's Parisian address and I've never heard a word from him since.'

Elinor, her story completed, sat back and contemplated her friend. Catriona was paying a fleeting visit to London so they had made hasty plans to have dinner together. Elinor had leaped at the chance to spill her heart out to her oldest and dearest friend and the response was everything she would have wished. Catriona had the fiery temperament that often went with red hair and her reaction was characteristically robust.

'Jean Pierre Pascal is a major love rat. You're well rid of him, Ellie!'

'I realise that now. Anyone who can leave a girl standing at the altar isn't worth a candle. But why didn't I see through his phoney charm? They say love is blind but I must have disengaged my brain whenever I was with him.'

'There was nothing to suggest he

would run out on you, was there?'

'Not really,' Elinor began hesitantly, 'but I did notice a subtle difference when Luc appeared on the scene. Jean Pierre was nervous around his brother and he seemed keen for us not to see too much of each other.'

'This is the Luc who virtually accused you of being after the family silver?'

'Well, he claimed that, after meeting me, he changed his mind.'

'That was generous of him!'

'That was my response, Cat. I'd just been brutally dumped and then I discover that my fiancé's family harboured all sorts of suspicions about me.'

A frown crossed Catriona's face.

'What do you know of the Pascal family?'

'Very little. Jean Pierre was quite reticent about his background. His parents' divorce and then the loss of his father seemed to have had quite a devastating impact on him, so I didn't probe too deeply.'

'Did he see much of his mother?'

'Apparently not,' Elinor said vaguely. 'She left France after the divorce and returned to the States leaving Jean Pierre and his brother with their father. The Pascals have some sort of estate south of Paris but I was never taken there.'

'Didn't you find that strange?'

Elinor's brow furrowed.

'On reflection, yes, but at the time I was so busy falling headlong in love with Jean Pierre I scarcely gave a thought to my prospective in-laws.'

Catriona's next question took her by surprise.

'And what do you know of Luc Pascal?'

'Not a great deal as it happens. Why?'

'It's just that he's making quite a splash in the French media at the moment as the government there has asked him to head some important trade negotiations.'

'Really? I know the Pascal family

business seems to have its fingers in all sorts of different ventures but I'd no idea Luc was so highly regarded by his own government.'

'Luc Pascal seems to be no ordinary businessman. He's been given these diplomatic rôles before.'

'How extraordinary. Jean Pierre never told me of his brother's exploits.'

But then there was much that Jean Pierre had kept hidden — like the fact that he was getting cold feet about their wedding!

'If Luc can cajole and negotiate for his country,' she added bitterly, 'breaking up me and Jean Pierre must have been easy in comparison!'

'You think Luc was behind his brother's change of heart?'

'I'm convinced of it. What other explanation could there be? Mind you . . . '

Her features broke into a sudden smile.

'I did, at least, have the satisfaction of lashing out at him. As Jean Pierre wasn't there he became the focus of all my anger and frustration. And I have no regrets about that, Cat. It was quite clear from his supercilious manner that he had never considered me good enough to grace the Pascal name!'

Elinor felt considerably better for this outburst and Catriona must have sensed that, too, for she moved the conversation on to the subject of Elinor's future.

'What are you going to do next, work wise,' she asked, 'now that your contract with the news agency has ended?'

Elinor's brow wrinkled.

'I'm not sure. I'm in contact with my old paper and I'll have to see what they can offer me, but let's not kid ourselves, Cat, I've let my career slide of late. I don't expect a dream assignment to just fall in my lap.'

She gazed down at her half-empty wine glass with an abstracted air, her words abrupt when she began again.

'You see, Jean Pierre wasn't keen on

my chosen career. He thought it would lead to too many separations, and he extracted a promise that I'd accept nothing which would take me from his side. Well, I don't need to worry about that now, do I? I can focus on my work without any distractions, because there's nothing in my life now but my career.'

This forced, brittle tone was most unlike her friend and as Catriona caught a glimpse of the suppressed pain in Elinor's eyes, she experienced a sudden rush of anger towards the absent Frenchman, and his brother, who had wrought such havoc in her best friend's life.

2

I think there might be an assignment for you, but we need to discuss it further. How about lunch next week?' Andrew said sympathetically when Elinor answered the phone.

'Of course,' Elinor returned swiftly. 'When and where?'

Andrew named a café bar close to the newspaper office and, when they had agreed on a day and time, he concluded with, 'I'm looking forward to seeing you, Ellie.'

My sentiments exactly, Elinor thought, as she replaced the receiver. Andrew had been out whenever she had phoned the office recently; and the suspicion had grown that he was avoiding her. But now he had contacted her, to hold out the enticing prospect of a job offer. Elinor's lips curved into a smile as she bent over her keyboard once more and resumed her typing.

On the appointed day, Elinor was first to arrive at the café. She looked up each time the swing door opened, the look of welcome on her face turning swiftly to disappointment. Where was Andrew? Although he was not noted for his punctuality it was unlike him to be quite so late and she experienced a stab of apprehension as she wondered if he was going to turn up at all. It wouldn't be just a missed appointment that would irk her. She was in urgent need of work and Andrew's phone call had raised hopes that he might be able to revive her flagging career. With her personal life in disarray her work now meant everything to her. It would be very hard to bear if that part of her life, too, was to fail.

'Ellie! I'm so sorry I'm late! Have you been waiting long?'

Elinor's eyes flew to Andrew's penitent face as he hovered at her side and she hastened to reassure him with a little white lie.

'I've not been here long, and I know how frantic things can get at the office, so I wasn't too worried when you weren't here on time.'

'I would have been early for once if I hadn't received a phone call from Paris just as I was ready to leave,' Andrew explained as he seated himself. 'As it concerned the assignment I want to discuss with you, I thought I'd better take it.'

A phone call from Paris? As Andrew turned aside to try and catch the eye of the waiter, questions teemed through Elinor's brain as she wondered if Andrew's job offer would result in her return to the French capital for, in spite of the poignant memories it evoked, it was still her dearest wish to return to France as a foreign correspondent.

Unfortunately, Andrew seemed in no hurry to satisfy her curiosity, perusing the menu at great length and asking the waiter about several dishes before finally opting for one. Then, their orders taken, the waiter scurried away and they were alone. Andrew pushed his spectacles up the bridge of his nose and, at last, came to the point.

'I'd like you to do an interview for me, Ellie. How do you feel about that?'

Slightly taken aback Elinor was unable to conceal her surprise.

'But I thought Lucy Taylor always did the interviews. How would she feel about me moving in on her territory?'

He dismissed her concerns with a wave of the hand.

'Oh, I've squared Lucy, so don't worry on that score. I want you for this job because I know you've been working in France and speak fluent French. You've got the right sort of background to put him at his ease.'

'Who?' Elinor asked, completely bewildered.

'Luc Pascal, the French businessman. Didn't I mention whom I want you to interview?'

As Elinor gave a silent shake of the head Andrew elaborated further.

'He's coming over to London in

about ten days, prior to his involvement in some important trade negotiations in Paris and that gives us the perfect opportunity to do a profile on him. Although he's well-known in France he's less well-known here. All that's set to change when he chairs these talks and we, much to our surprise, have been offered an exclusive interview. It's a real coup, Ellie, and I think you're the best person to handle it.'

There was no doubting the enthusiasm in his voice, and Elinor hated to disappoint him, but there was no way she could meet Luc Pascal.

'I'm sorry, Andrew, but I don't want this assignment. It's out of the question.'

Andrew's face was a picture of dismay.

'But, why? You've been badgering me for work for ages and now you're turning down a great job offer. I simply don't understand, Ellie.'

In the face of Andrew's incredulity she almost blurted out the truth, that

Luc Pascal had ruined her life and she could not meet him again without reliving the agony of her greatest humiliation, but thankfully, her natural caution held her back. Andrew knew nothing about the turmoil in her private life and she preferred to keep it that way.

Breaking the silence she said, 'There are personal reasons for my refusal which I just can't go into. I'm truly grateful for all you're trying to do for me, but I think it would be a lot better if you sent Lucy to do this interview.'

'But I've chosen you!' Andrew rapped out his reply. 'And I must say I find your attitude very disappointing. When you first came to me as a cub reporter I hope I imbued you with a strong sense of professionalism. Vague personal reasons are no excuse for turning down the chance to do an interview which it has taken me considerable time and trouble to set up!'

His scathing response took Elinor

completely by surprise and stung by this attack on her professionalism, she found herself at a loss as to how to respond. Just then the waiter arrived with their meals and Elinor was thankful for the interruption, thoughts racing through her brain as she wondered how to pacify Andrew. She simply couldn't afford to upset him. She was far too reliant on his goodwill for further work. And his words had been a forceful reminder that a good journalist should not let personal considerations interfere with their work.

Taking a deep breath Elinor said, 'Look, if you really think it's important that I do this interview, then, of course I'll do it.'

Andrew's smile stretched to the far corners of his eyes.

'Good girl! I knew you'd see sense. Come into the office tomorrow and I'll get the business desk to furnish you with all the background details. But, remember, I don't want just a dry, business profile. I really want us to get under the skin of Luc Pascal and find out what makes him tick.'

Having met the enigmatic Frenchman Elinor feared that was an impossible task but now that she was committed to the assignment she made a silent vow to execute it to the very best of her ability.

A week later, standing nervously in the lobby of the hotel where she was to meet Luc, her hand tightened unconsciously on her valise as she consoled herself with the thought that at least she was thoroughly prepared for the interview ahead. Extensive research in the newspaper's files had provided her with enough material for a dozen interviews but when this had been whittled down to a series of concise questions and these had been approved by Luc's Parisian office, she felt confident that her time with Luc would be productive, but brief.

'Elinor! How delightful to see you again!'

Elinor turned at the sound of his

distinctive voice to find him standing beside her, immaculately dressed, as always, in a charcoal grey suit, dazzling white shirt, and silk tie in navy. Taking her cue from him, that they were simply old friends meeting up, she touched the extended hand briefly and said, a little breathlessly, 'And it's nice to see you again, Luc.'

She was surprised by his aplomb. As his office had approved her appointment she could only suppose that Luc was unfazed by their re-union after their last stormy meeting, which only served to confirm the man's insensitivity, she concluded sourly, following him into the ante-room which had been put at their disposal.

As she settled on the Chesterfield sofa and retrieved her tape recorder and notes from her briefcase she declined Luc's offer of coffee.

'No refreshments, thank you. I'd be quite happy to start the interview straight away.'

'Whatever you wish, Elinor.'

He settled himself opposite, his expression unreadable as she switched on her tape recorder and began. In spite of her initial nervousness she soon realised that Luc Pascal was as adept at interviews as he seemed to be in every other area of his life. Clearly he had already studied the questions passed on to his office and the replies sprang readily to his lips, fluent and concise. About an hour later, Elinor was switching off her tape recorder and leaning back, one hand rubbing at the back of her neck as she realised that her ordeal was over. She couldn't help throwing Luc a look of gratitude.

'I think my editor will be well pleased with that, Luc,' she said. 'Thank you for your co-operation. I am grateful, you know.'

'I will do anything to help you, Elinor.'

The words were spoken with sincerity and when Elinor was subjected to one of Luc's charming smiles she felt the colour flood into her cheeks.

Reaching forward for her valise, her hair swung forward to hide her face and it was a moment or two before Luc's next words sank in.

'You want me to dine with you?' she repeated, her voice rising on a note of incredulity.

'The hotel cuisine is highly recommended,' he explained patiently, 'and I would consider it an honour if you would join me for dinner.'

'But I'm not really dressed for dining out,' Elinor stammered, searching feverishly for an excuse.

'You look perfectly charming.'

His glance swept over her, taking in the well-cut linen suit in a soft blue which went so well with her dark colouring.

'Of course,' he added, a derisive smile playing about his lips, 'you may well have a prior engagement.'

It was the perfect excuse and, as Elinor opened her mouth to take it, she hesitated momentarily, and then found herself saying, 'As it happens, I am free, and I'd like to accept your invitation.'

Surprise fleeted across his face and then he was standing up.

'Come, Elinor. The head waiter has reserved a very fine table for me and we must go quickly, before he gives it to another eager client.'

As she followed him from the room Elinor berated herself inwardly for rashly agreeing to spend the evening with him, still not quite sure why she had accepted so easily. What would they talk about — her life since his brother had brutally dumped her? Her nervous tension threatened to turn into giggles and when the head waiter engaged Luc in a brief conversation in rapid French she took the opportunity to compose her features before following Luc across the crowded dining-room to a small, round table set in an alcove formed by a bay window. The table centrepiece of pearly white roses sent out a subtle fragrance as Luc drew out Elinor's chair.

'This is charming,' Elinor commented as she settled herself.

'The food is good, too,' Luc confirmed, handing over a menu.

Elinor took her time choosing, keen to delay the moment when she would have to sit back and make small talk with a man she had vowed never to speak to again. It was Luc who broke the silence with a comment about an exhibition he had managed to see earlier in the day. As Elinor had recently seen the same exhibition this led to a lively discussion about its merits, Luc making wildly provocative statements which Elinor was forced to counter. At last she held up one hand as though to stem his flow of words.

'I don't think you believe a single word you're saying,' she protested. 'You're just out to tease me.'

Luc raised his glass of wine in a mock toast.

'And why not, Elinor, when it brings such a delightful colour to your cheeks?'

The blush deepened as Elinor concentrated on her meal but Luc now changed tack, embarking on a stream of amusing anecdotes to demonstrate the differences between English and French customs. It was difficult not to respond to his banter and by the end of the meal Elinor could only marvel that she and Luc had just spent several hours together without mentioning anything controversial or personal.

Gazing down abstractedly at her coffee cup as she stirred the rich, dark liquid, she couldn't help putting some of her thoughts into words.

'I wish I had seen this side to you before, Luc. You seem so relaxed.'

And quite charming, she added inwardly, still bemused at the skilful way Luc had managed to neutralise her hostility. His gaze shifted from hers and his expression was unreadable as he looked down at his coffee cup.

'I think that is a polite way of saying I am not quite the villain you thought I was.'

Now it was Elinor's turn to gaze downwards.

'I don't think that's quite fair,' she murmured at last. 'It wasn't you who left me at the altar.'

'But you still blame me for Jean Pierre's decision?'

She looked up, their eyes locking, as she sought for the right words.

'It's difficult for me not to feel resentment towards you,' she admitted candidly, 'when I know full well that you doubted my motives in wanting to marry Jean Pierre.'

He inclined his dark head towards her.

'When you asked me what I had thought about your marriage to my brother I tried to be honest but, instead, I fear I was merely tactless. My apologies, Elinor, for making things worse at a very painful time for you.'

It was a graceful acknowledgement of his clumsy behaviour, but the awkward fact remained that he had mistrusted her!

'It was a difficult time for both of us,' she murmured at last.

Suddenly she was unwilling to probe further into an event which had turned her life upside down and cost her many hours of sleep.

Squaring her shoulders, she said, 'But it's pointless dwelling on the past, Luc. Whatever happened, happened. It's time to look forward.'

'Ah, yes, the future. And what are your plans, Elinor?'

'Well, there's my career, of course. I'm still interested in working as a foreign correspondent and I have hopes that Andrew, my editor, will be able to find something for me soon.'

'Of course, but it can be a lonely life for a woman, moving from post to post. Is a rootless existence what you really want, Elinor?'

'A settled life isn't really an option at the moment,' she couldn't help pointing out, astonished by his remarks.

What right had Luc to comment on the choices she was making, when his brother had just ripped her life apart? He had the grace to look a little ashamed.

'Once more I have been tactless, Elinor! I am so sorry, and, truly, I wish only the best for you.'

Mollified, Elinor picked up her coffee cup, toying with it as she said, 'I think Andrew will be well pleased with the interview when I've written it up.'

She tipped back her head to drink the last of her coffee, replaced the cup on the saucer and commented, 'I must say I was surprised when Andrew said you'd agreed to an interview. I thought you normally avoided publicity.'

'Sometimes it is necessary.'

He shrugged, glancing aside, but not before Elinor had detected a wariness in his eyes which caused suspicion in her mind. She remained silent whilst he made a show of drinking his coffee and then she spoke.

'Luc, you asked for me specifically to do this interview, didn't you?'

He went very still, colour rising

beneath his tanned cheeks as Elinor drew in her breath sharply. No wonder Andrew had been so insistent she take the assignment. No doubt Luc had made it a condition of granting the interview. She'd been set up. And she knew by whom!

'Jean Pierre told you to do this, didn't he?' she insisted heatedly. 'He thinks he owes me because of his appalling behaviour and he wants to put some work my way.'

'Jean Pierre? What has he to do with this?'

Luc threw down his crumpled-up napkin with a sigh of exasperation and leaned back in his chair, one hand jerking through his dark hair.

'For your information I haven't seen my brother since he ran out on you. I don't know where he is or what he is doing.'

The expression on Elinor's face turned swiftly from anger to surprise.

'But he works for the family business.'

'Not any more. A letter of resignation was faxed to our head office, but there was no contact number on it and no one in the family has heard from him since.'

'But aren't you going to look for him?'

'No. He is a grown man. If he wishes to disappear from our lives, so be it,' Luc said bleakly.

Once more Elinor had the strong feeling that Luc was hiding something from her but she had to concede. The fraught relationship between the two brothers was no longer her concern. It was her fraught relationship with Luc she now had to deal with!

'So,' she said, breaking the ensuing silence, 'drawing me into this interview was all your idea, Luc.'

'For my sins, it was. I believed the Pascal family owed you something and I wanted to help you resume your career.'

'But I wanted to do that on my own merits. Can't you see that?'

Making no attempt to mask her anger, she glared at him, unable to resist a last barb.

'At one time you thought I wanted the Pascal name for the influence it would bring me. You were wrong then and you're wrong now in thinking I would ever want any help from you.'

He looked taken aback at her response, saying stiffly, 'I am sorry I have upset you, Elinor. I meant everything for the best, truly I did.'

Looking at the pained expression on his face Elinor let out a heavy sigh. He just didn't understand, did he? Her self-esteem had taken a huge knock when his brother had walked out on her and now she'd discovered that this plum assignment was down to Luc's influence rather than her own abilities. Was there no end to the damage the Pascal brothers were going to inflict? Reaching across she touched him briefly on the hand, her tone a little more conciliatory.

'I accept you thought you were doing

the right thing but it's important that I re-establish my life on my own. There isn't any part you can play.'

He inclined his dark head in tacit acknowledgement of her words and then she was walking away from him, head high, and inwardly expressing the wish that her involvement with the Pascal family was well and truly over.

* * *

'Congratulations, Ellie. Your interview with Luc Pascal is just what I was looking for, informative without being too dry. We'll showcase it in our weekend supplement. It should get you a lot of attention.'

Elinor found herself exhaling sharply. When Andrew had called her and invited her to lunch the thought had immediately crossed her mind that her article had not found favour and he had decided to see her away from the office so as not to embarrass her in front of colleagues when he poured scorn on her efforts.

All this must have been evident on her face for Andrew, noted for his plain speaking, prompted her out of her silence with, 'I caught you out there, didn't I, Ellie? You thought I'd brought you here to trash your article.'

'Yes!' Elinor's smile broadened. 'I must admit I thought lunch out with you was a consolation prize for some tough talking. I'm very glad I was wrong,' she added. 'Your approval means a good deal to me, Andrew.'

'So it should do,' he returned, his brusqueness of tone belied by the twinkle in his grey eyes. 'I've been in the business since before you were born, my girl, and I know a good journalist when I see one. You have talent, Ellie, and with greater experience and a little more faith in yourself you should do very well in this business. Now, I'm wondering what I should do with you next. Any suggestions?'

Elinor had, and she knew the time

was right, now that Andrew was in this expansive mood, to make a bold suggestion.

'My heart's still set on being a foreign correspondent and I did wonder if there were any openings in France.'

Andrew's response was swift.

'I'm afraid that's impossible, Ellie. Gerry Fitzpatrick is firmly ensconced in Paris and the budget won't run to two journalists there. Look, I know you're disappointed but there are other jobs you could consider. I expect the Far Eastern desk to have a vacancy quite soon. Terry Bell is getting rather tired of the rat race in Hong Kong and wants to return to Europe.'

'How soon exactly might there be a vacancy?'

'Christmas, probably,' Andrew said vaguely. 'But I'm sure I can find some assignments to keep you busy until then. I'll give it some thought and get in touch within the next few days. Will you be in London?'

'No,' Elinor said, coming to a sudden

decision. 'Contact me at home.'

If there was to be a lull in her work she may as well return to the Cotswolds and spend some time with her father.

* ★ ★

Elinor fed the last sheet of paper into the fax machine, glanced out through the window and, enticed by the brilliant blue sky, ran down the stairs and through the open front door into the garden. The heat hit her and she slowed down to follow the gravel path which skirted the house and then led through the back garden into a wooded area of deep shade.

'There you are, Ellie,' her father stated, lowering his glass of iced lemonade as she approached.

He was seated at a sun-dappled table beneath an oak tree. He cast her a questioning look as she joined him.

'Have you finished the piece you were working on?'

'Yes,' she said. 'It didn't require

much effort. Domestic issues rarely do in my experience.'

As she lapsed into silence, James Dale wondered what to say next. Although her editor was passing commissions her way he knew it was the sort of lightweight work which she really wasn't interested in.

'Perhaps you'd be better off in London, love. It'd be easier to keep up the pressure on Andrew if you were on the spot,' he said in an effort to be constructive.

He had a point. If she stayed buried in the countryside much longer she might be reduced to reporting on the village fête for the local rag! But the solution to her problem could not be resolved by changing her location.

'I doubt if it would make any difference,' she told her father. 'I'm sure Andrew is doing his best for me but the openings just aren't there at the moment. Besides, there are practical difficulties about returning to London. Cassie's got a cousin staying with her at

51

the moment and I can hardly suggest she threw her out just so that I can have my old room back.'

When Elinor was in London she usually stayed with an old school friend. Mostly it worked out well but it was an informal arrangement and Elinor accepted that there were times when her friend needed the room for someone else.

They lapsed into silence and Elinor, feeling restless, decided on action. Jumping to her feet she declared her intention of walking to the village to buy a newspaper and then strode off, leaving her father to stare at her retreating back, a frown settling on his brow as he wondered when his sensitive, creative daughter would be able to throw off the shadows of the past and pick up the pieces of her life once more.

She was working on some ideas that evening when her father called upstairs.

'Ellie! Phone call for you. It's Catriona!'

Elinor came tearing down the stairs to take the receiver from her father.

'Cat, hi! It's wonderful to hear from you.'

Catriona had been rather incommunicado recently and Elinor's implicit rebuke brought an immediate response.

'Sorry I've not been in touch. I've been up to my ears in helping Reynaldi prepare for his autumn collection and when I've finished a long day at work I just come home again and sleep! Anyway, we're through the worst now. I'm ready to start living again, and you, Ellie, dear, are part of the plan.'

'That sounds promising! Tell me more!'

'How about a trip to Paris? I've got a spare bedroom, some free time now, and an urge to go gallivanting with my best friend. What do you say?'

'Yes,' Elinor said promptly.

Laughter bubbled along the line.

'You sound as though you need a holiday as much as I do!'

'I certainly do, and it will be lovely to

see you again and catch up on the news. So, when would you like me to come?'

'How about Friday? There's a shuttle flight late afternoon and if you take a cab from the airport you can be at my place by early evening.'

Excitedly Elinor agreed, promising to call when she had made her final arrangements, then, replacing the receiver, she set off to find her father to tell him the good news.

3

The cab screeched to a sudden halt, throwing Elinor forward. As she attempted to regain her balance she found the door opening as the driver reached in to collect her suitcase with one hand and help her out with the other. She looked around, taking stock.

She was in a boulevard typical of the Western fringes of central Paris. Horse chestnuts, in straight lines, bordered the pavements and the buildings all shared the same elegant, classical proportions, with decorative wrought iron balcony railings, ornamental carvings around the double doorways and arched windows. She hurried up the stone steps in front of her to look for Catriona's name on the list of residents. There it was, in the neat italic script which they had both been taught at school. She pressed the buzzer and

Catriona's voice crackled out of the intercom.

'I saw you arrive, Ellie. Come on up, the door's open.'

The door swung to at her touch and she was drawn into a cool, dark hallway with potted palms in brass planters, a marble floor of mottled grey and walls painted in the faded green so typical of Parisian apartment houses. Catriona was situated on the top floor and by the time she had carried her suitcase up several storeys, Elinor was glad to see an open doorway and Catriona's smiling figure on the threshold.

'Hey, let me take that.'

Catriona grimaced as she collected the suitcase from her friend.

'What on earth have you got in this?'

'Rather a lot of clothes,' Elinor admitted, a little shamefaced. 'We hadn't really decided how long I should stay so I brought plenty.'

Catriona dropped the suitcase just inside the door and deposited a kiss on her friend's cheek.

'You can stay as long as you like, Ellie. It's great having you.'

Elinor expressed the frustration of the past few weeks in a heartfelt sigh.

'You don't know how pleased I am to be here!'

As Catriona disappeared into the small kitchen to make some coffee Elinor wandered around the sitting-room, comfortably furnished with two large couches adorned by colourful scatter cushions with covers designed by Catriona. Elinor approved of all she saw. Anyone would recognise this room as belonging to someone creative and successful, and she couldn't help feeling a momentary pang that her best friend's career seemed to be reaching a new high just as hers was stalling.

Appalled at the turn her thoughts were taking she admonished herself for her moment of self pity and then crossed over to the large picture windows through which the early evening sun poured.

'Aren't they glorious?'

Catriona, who had just entered the room, jerked her head in the direction of the windows.

'These apartments were converted from artists' studios which dominated this neighbourhood in the mid-nineteenth century and those huge windows were designed to allow the maximum of northern light in.'

'Luxury apartments for artists? You mean not all of them starved in garrets?' Elinor quipped as she wandered over to join her friend.

'Not the ones who lived here, anyway!'

Catriona handed a cup of coffee over and then settled herself on one of the couches.

Elinor sat opposite, drank a little of the steaming brew, then commented, 'I'm really pleased to see you so well settled here. You have a lovely home and, clearly, your work is going well.'

Catriona pulled a face.

'Reynaldi does have me tearing my hair out at times, you know! It's not all sweetness and light but, on the whole, I guess I am quite contented.'

She replaced her cup and saucer on the coffee table then subjected her friend to a quizzical glance.

'Unlike you, Ellie. I'm getting the distinct impression that you were quite desperate to have a break from home. What on earth is wrong?'

Trust Catriona to come straight to the point!

'I'm not using you as a bolt hole,' she insisted, 'but, yes, I was ready for a change of scene.'

She told Catriona about her lack of work.

'My career seems to be at a standstill and I don't really know what to do about it,' she concluded.

'Is there any chance your editor might assign you to this trade conference which is getting so much media coverage? After all you're here now, on the spot.'

'I don't think Andrew takes much notice of my holiday destinations! The

Paris correspondent will cover it as part of his normal duties.'

'Can't you do some freelance work on it whilst you're here?'

'It's difficult without official clearance. I wouldn't be allowed into the daily Press briefings.'

There was a brief pause and then Catriona surprised her by saying, 'What about Luc Pascal? He's at the heart of these negotiations and he's rarely off the television giving his views on their progress. Can't he help you in some way? After all, he gave you an interview not long ago.'

Elinor had only given brief details of her encounter with Luc to her friend and her voice was tight when she replied.

'It was Andrew who persuaded me to do that interview, Cat, and I wasn't best pleased when I discovered that Luc had put him up to it.'

'But why? It was a great coup for you; and you've just been saying that your career needs a boost. It's only right that Luc Pascal should help you out. That family owes you.'

'They owe me nothing! The last thing I want is to be patronised by the elder brother after being dumped by the younger one!'

Her anger vanished as suddenly as it had flared up and she leaned back against the cushions.

'Look, I'm sorry I snapped just now but the fact is that nothing will induce me to use my contacts with Luc to further my career. There are too many barriers between us for relations to be cordial.'

'I still think he could be of use to you,' Catriona repeated, adding daringly, 'You can't be certain he blocked your marriage.'

'I can't be certain of anything because I was never given a satisfactory explanation, but what happened will always mar my relationship with Luc and when we parted in London we made no plans to meet again. I certainly won't be seeking him out to ask for favours.'

Catriona realised it would be futile to pursue the subject any longer and, changing tack, she asked Elinor what she would like to do during her visit. They spent the next hour working out an itinerary for sightseeing.

The next week was a whirlwind of activity as the two friends caught up with the latest exhibitions, saw a show which had transferred from New York, revisited some of the more famous sights and enjoyed eating out in some of the noted bistros in Catriona's neighbourhood.

Since coming to live in Paris Catriona had made many friends, and the weekend beckoned enticingly with an invitation to a party at an art gallery to celebrate a new exhibition by an up-and-coming artist.

'Robert really is a fine artist,' Catriona enthused, 'specialising in oils. He's designing the sets for Reynaldi's next show so we've got to know each other quite well. Everyone from work is going to his party and we thought we'd all go out to dinner afterwards.'

It sounded as though it was going to be great fun and the only question Elinor had was, what was she going to wear? Catriona's answer was blithely confident.

'Whatever you like, Ellie. You'll look great, as you always do.'

Elinor was not so sure and pored over the clothes she had brought, finally opting for a dress in navy velvet, strapless, with a fitted bodice and a short skirt. Dark stockings and shoes with spiky heels completed the outfit but when she joined Catriona in the sitting-room on Saturday evening she took one look at her friend and exclaimed, 'I'm dressed far too formally! I'll change into something else.'

'Don't you dare!' Catriona warned.

Resplendent in a floor-length gown, caftan-style, in a kingfisher blue which formed a vivid contrast with her red hair, she cut a striking figure, and her eyes were now trained professionally on her friend.

'I'm a dress designer, I'm supposed to break all the rules,' she went on dismissively, 'but you, Ellie, are not, and you have wisely chosen a dress that is right for you. One thing's for sure, though. It'll make male heads turn!'

Elinor knew her friend was only trying to boost her ego.

'You could do with a splash of colour, though. Hang on a minute.'

She disappeared, only to return a moment later with a long, thin scarf in a vivid blue, shot through with a silver thread.

'It's pure silk and was a present from Reynaldi,' she said as she wound it around Elinor's neck.

'It's beautiful. You were right, it does add something.'

The small, exclusive gallery on the Left Bank was very crowded, with people spilling out on to the pavement, and shortly after Catriona introduced her to Robert Braque she realised that

64

he and Catriona were a little more than good friends as he swept her off to meet the rest of his guests. Elinor was left to her own devices and, as she knew few people there, was relieved when she fell into conversation with a Canadian, Jake Taylor, a gallery owner himself who was on a buying trip.

He seemed adept at negotiating the scrum to collect glasses of sparkling wine from the waiters and as Elinor drank one glass after another and listened to his amusing anecdotes about his business dealings in Paris, she began to feel very relaxed. Instead of the crowd thinning, though, it seemed to be getting worse. Elinor hadn't seen Catriona for some time and when Jake suggested they leave the gallery and find somewhere to eat she was sorely tempted.

'I really ought to speak to my friend,' she demurred. 'I think she was expecting us to eat together.'

Catriona was nowhere to be found, however, and as Elinor was now feeling the pangs of hunger, she waylaid a woman she recognised as one of her friend's colleagues and asked her to pass on a message. On returning to Jake she told him that she could now accept his kind invitation to dine, and they set off into the night.

They were able to hail a cab quite quickly and, on Jake's instructions, the driver departed for his hotel.

'The Hotel Belvedere is noted for its cuisine,' he told her. 'Good, country cooking, French food at its best.'

It was certainly a charming, turn-of-the-century building and as the head waiter escorted them across a deep-piled carpet, sprinkled with tiny golden stars, to a small table in the corner Elinor felt confident that she was in for a pleasurable evening. An hour later she was not so sure. The food, certainly, was delicious but as the meal had worn on and Jake had drunk more, his manner had become increasingly objectionable and Elinor began to regret her rather rash decision to go out to dinner with a man she hardly knew.

His hand clamped over hers.

'We could continue this conversation in my room, honey.'

Elinor pulled her hand free and tried to instil some regret into her voice.

'I'm sorry, Jake, but it's getting late and my friend will be wondering where I am. I think I should be getting back.'

An ugly flush spread over his face.

'But you're a grown woman. You're not a kid, honey, who's on a curfew. What are you trying to say here?'

Suddenly losing patience Elinor picked up her handbag and stood up.

'I'm trying to say that I'm leaving, right now. Thank you for the meal but I must say good-night.'

As she turned to go he made one last effort to detain her but as his hand curled around her arm and he swung her round to face him, he swayed forward slightly and the contents of the full glass of wine in his left hand poured down the front of her dress. Elinor looked down in horror at the spreading stain whilst Jake flapped his hands beside her.

'Oh, I'm sorry. Hang on whilst I get a cloth or something.'

He stumbled off but Elinor had no intention of waiting and, turning on her heels, she stalked out of the dining-room. The doorman was talking to the receptionist and, at her request, he went outside to look for a cab for her. As she waited she began to pace up and down, reflecting ruefully on her disastrous evening. Not only had she spent most of the last hour fending off the attentions of a man whose manners seemed to have deteriorated with every sip of wine but, if she didn't get home soon and attend to her dress, she faced the prospect of it being ruined for good.

'There you are, honey.'

She turned in surprise to find herself facing Jake, who was brandishing some sort of dishcloth. As he made a movement towards her she stepped back automatically.

'Don't look at me like that, as though

I'm dirt beneath your feet.'

His hands gripped her upper arms.

'I bought you a darned fine dinner tonight. The least you can do is show me some gratitude.'

Elinor found herself being hauled towards him, his alcoholic laden breath juddering against her cheeks as she squeezed her eyes tight shut before the inevitable impact of his lips on hers. Next moment a familiar, autocratic voice was berating Jake for his appalling manners and, as his hands fell, releasing her, she opened her eyes to find herself facing Luc Pascal!

4

Jake's surprise at being censured by a perfect stranger now turned to anger and, his chin jutting out, he stared at Luc belligerently.

'Who said you could push your nose in? How I talk to my date is none of your darned business so you can just butt out, mister.'

Elinor looked anxiously across at the desk to see if a member of staff could come to their aid, only to find it deserted. Meanwhile, Luc, his expression impenetrable, took one menacing step forward.

'It is my concern, monsieur, when I see a man treat a woman with all the contempt you have just displayed and if you don't want to face a complaint for assault, I suggest that you make yourself scarce, immediately.'

Jake opened his mouth as though to

continue the dispute and then all the fight seemed to go out of him and, muttering beneath his breath, he slunk away. Elinor then found herself the focus of Luc's dark eyes. Deeply embarrassed she began an explanation.

He brushed aside her words.

'I could see what was happening, Elinor. There is no need to explain.'

His eyes lowered to take in the stained bodice of her dress.

'Your dress will be ruined if we do not do something quickly.'

He took hold of her arm, speaking as they went.

'You can change in my room and I will get the hotel valet service to see to your dress.'

Elinor was too astonished to question Luc's commands and she found herself being led to the first floor where Luc's suite was. After stepping inside she hardly had time to take in the features of the room before she was bundled into the bathroom with a request to remove her dress!

I must be mad to have agreed to this, she thought, as she slipped out of the garment. Not that Luc had given her much choice! In his usual high-handed manner he had simply taken control, and she couldn't help feeling annoyed with herself that she had let him. Opening the door, she peeked around it and then passed out the dress to Luc's waiting hand. There was a robe hanging on the back of the door and she pulled it on and then crossed to the mirror to view her reflection. The robe was far too large so she rolled back the sleeves and wound the belt twice around her waist, fastening it securely. Wide blue eyes stared back at her, outlined by smudged mascara, so she ran some water into the bowl and gave her face a thorough wash.

The sophisticated, upswept style of her hair which Catriona had created for her earlier was now in a sorry state so she pulled out the pins and shook her head until her hair tumbled loose upon her shoulders. She checked her appearance once more in the mirror and was relieved to see that every vestige of her earlier self had gone. She wished she could remove every trace of the disastrous evening just as easily.

Luc was seated on a chaise longue when she joined him, his long legs stretched out in front of him, his discarded dinner jacket to one side and his white silk shirt open at the neck, giving him a slightly rakish air.

'You're out of the bathroom at last,' he remarked as she sat opposite in a high-backed chair. 'I thought you were going to hide in there all night.

Elinor decided to ignore this provocation.

'I suppose I must thank you for your intervention,' she went on, although she couldn't help adding, 'But there was no real need, you know. I'm a grown woman. I do know how to handle drunken louts.'

'Date many of them, do you?'

Elinor felt the colour rise in her cheeks.

'No, I do not! You are deliberately misunderstanding me,' she accused.

'I know, but I cannot resist teasing you!'

Elinor's colour deepened as he went on.

'But it is remarkable, is it not, how we have met by chance? Are you by any chance following me, Elinor?'

Elinor tossed her head.

'I could accuse you of the same thing!'

'Oh, Elinor.'

Luc was leaning forward, a provocative edge to his voice.

'If I was pursuing you, you would be well aware of the fact.'

Shooting him a suspicious glance, Elinor detected amusement in the depths of his dark eyes. Just as she had thought — he was trying to capitalise on her discomfort by embarking on foolish games! Well, she would not be drawn into a sparring match for Luc Pascal's entertainment and, shifting her eyes from his, her voice deliberately toneless, she asked him how long it would be before her dress was returned.

'Oh, you will not have to suffer my company for very long, Elinor. The valet service is very quick. Still, we will have time for a drink, so, what can I get for you?'

'Just coffee, please.'

Her head had started to thump uncomfortably and she cursed herself for the reckless way in which she had downed several glasses of champagne at the art gallery. If she'd had a clear head she was sure she would never have been taken in by the loathsome Jake, in which case she wouldn't now be sitting in a robe in Luc's room and subject to his snide comments.

'Is it too much to ask what you are doing in Paris?'

Luc turned aside from the coffee machine to throw her a quizzical glance.

'Or will that result in a caustic comment to mind my business?'

'It's no secret,' she said defensively.

'I'm here on holiday, staying with my friend, Catriona.'

Dark brows rose as he handed over her coffee.

'Really? I'd assumed you were here to cover the trade conference for your newspaper.'

'I'm afraid not. Andrew has a correspondent who's reported on these things for the last three decades! It's a plum assignment and not intended for someone at the start of their career.'

It was difficult to keep the bitterness out of her voice and, aware that she had revealed more than she had intended, she chewed absentmindedly at her lower lip. When he spoke his voice was sympathetic.

'You must be very disappointed.'

'That's an understatement, Luc.'

There was a strained silence which Elinor broke.

'You must be finding the whole thing very time consuming, Luc, as Catriona tells me that you're at the heart of these negotiations.'

'For my sins, I am, Elinor.'

From the weary tone of his voice she gathered that they were not going well and when he elaborated by telling her that they often worked well into the night, she concluded that this must account for his rather dishevelled appearance.

As though sensing her thoughts he added, 'This is a rare night off for me, Elinor, so it is a bonus to spend part of it with someone as charming and lovely as you.'

Elinor made no attempt at a reply and began to drink her coffee. As they sat in silence she was alive to the fact that she was quite exhausted and wanted nothing more of the evening than to return to Catriona's apartment and go to bed. As she attempted to stifle a yawn, there came a knock at the door and when Luc opened it there as a rapid exchange in French.

He returned empty-handed and, at Elinor's questioning look, explained.

'Your dress will not be ready until the

morning, Elinor, so you will have to spend the night here.'

As Elinor gaped at him, he went on.

'You cannot travel across Paris dressed in a man's robe and, as I do not have any women's clothing to offer you, it seems like the best solution!'

'I was just wondering where I was going to sleep.'

'Here!'

With an impatient gesture he rose and flung open a door in the far wall and Elinor crossed over to peek into a large room, her eyes immediately drawn to a huge bed set against the wall with an oyster-coloured satin coverlet and heart-shaped cushions decorating the head rest.

'It has its own facilities,' he said, jerking his head in the direction of a cream-painted door. 'I am sure you will be very comfortable.'

'But where will you sleep?' she queried.

'On the couch, of course.'

'Oh, no. I'll take that, it's only fair.'

'Elinor, take the bed. I have been deprived of so much sleep recently, I would be able to sleep on bare boards.'

She opened her mouth to protest once more and he laid one finger warningly against her lips. That simple gesture sent a shock pulsing through her and in the stillness that followed she could feel every unsteady beat of her heart. Time seemed suspended and, acutely aware of the unspoken query in the dark depths of his eyes, a shiver of anticipation went through her, to be quickly followed by doubt and uncertainty. His eyes tracked the conflicting emotions fleeting across her face and gentle hands cradled her face, his fingers winding through the silky tresses of her hair.

'Do not look so fearful, Elinor. I ask of you nothing that you do not give willingly, with the whole for your heart.'

Then his lips were moving against hers in a gentle, tender kiss, so at odds with his usually assertive manner that Elinor was, momentarily, beguiled into a response. It was a mistake. The kiss deepened and Elinor found herself tensing, suddenly aware of the folly of what she was doing.

He released her immediately, a rueful smile crossing his face as he turned away with the words, 'Good-night, Elinor.'

Murmuring her reply, Elinor slipped into the bedroom and after showering, she curled up in the huge bed, convinced she would be unable to sleep but, just as she was attempting to make sense of the unsettling events of the evening, sleep claimed her.

As sunlight crept through the voile curtains to stir her gently into wakefulness, the more raucous noises of early-morning Paris added a discordant note and she found herself coming to with a shock. As memories of the previous evening flooded into her mind, she sat upright, only to sink back abruptly as a tap came at the door and Luc's voice asked if he could come in. She called out her permission and the door was flung open to reveal Luc carrying a breakfast tray, with her dress folded over one arm.

'Coffee and fresh croissants, and some clothes to wear,' he added, as he dropped her dress on to the bed.

Elinor thanked him and when he had left she threw the bedclothes back and padded across to the shower room. Hot needles of water brought her to full wakefulness and, after breakfasting and dressing, she went through into the sitting-room to find Luc glancing impatiently at his watch.

'There you are. I have an official car waiting downstairs ready to take you home.'

He was now every inch the businessman and spent all of their journey time to her apartment on his car phone. When they finally drew to a halt outside, he broke off his conversation only briefly to bid her a quick, 'Au revoir, Elinor.'

She responded in kind as she clambered out and the car drove off.

Her hand rose to her neck to flick her hair back, only to freeze as it suddenly dawned on her that Catriona's scarf was not there. She must have left it at Luc's, and the darned thing had been a present from Reynaldi! Cursing inwardly, Elinor let herself in with the key Catriona had given her and set off for the top floor. The door swung open at her approach to reveal her friend, still in her robe, looking as though she had had little sleep.

'Ellie, thank goodness! I was worried sick about you. Where on earth have you been?'

Elinor brushed past her with the words, 'Don't ask!' and as she disappeared into her room to change, Catriona was left staring at the closed door, her mouth open.

Elinor did tell her friend the whole sorry saga later, after she had changed into a T-shirt and jeans and they were sharing a pot of tea.

'I must have been crazy to have gone off with a man I hardly knew,' she concluded. 'He turned into a monster once we were alone together.'

That was not the part of the story which intrigued Catriona.

'Oh, we all make that sort of mistake from time to time,' she said blithely. 'More to the point, what about you and Luc?'

'What about us?' Elinor repeated sharply. 'Nothing happened.'

'I wasn't suggesting otherwise, Ellie! I just think it's rather strange that you two should bump into each other.'

'Unfortunate, certainly, as I was being pawed by Jake when Luc happened by. It gave him the chance to act out the white knight when, of course, I could have handled everything myself.'

'Of course,' Catriona agreed solemnly.

Choosing to ignore the hint of amusement in her friend's eyes, Elinor continued with, 'Well, this time I do expect my parting from Luc to be final.'

There was, of course, the problem of

Catriona's missing scarf and, as she hadn't yet summoned up the courage to tell her friend of the loss, she was in a quandary as to what to do about it. She really did not want to make contact with Luc again but if she had left the scarf in his hotel suite, that was the only way she was going to retrieve it.

As it happened, her problem was solved that very evening when she opened the door to a young man who handed her a bouquet of one dozen red roses. Intertwined with the stems was Catriona's scarf and she had just disentangled it when her friend walked into the room.

'Wow! Are they for you, Ellie?' she exclaimed.

'Yes, they're from Luc.'

As she pulled the gold-edged card from the envelope, Catriona gazed curiously over her shoulder. His italic script, so like his brother's, relayed the request, *Dine with me?* It was unsigned but there was a telephone number neatly printed in the bottom, right-hand corner.

'That man really has style,' Catriona said admiringly. 'You are going to go out with him, aren't you?'

'Perhaps,' Elinor murmured.

She slipped the card into the pocket of her jeans, knowing that she had no intention of taking him up on his invitation but was unwilling to rouse her friend's ire by dismissing it out of hand.

Over the next week, Elinor and Catriona resumed their sightseeing and, thankfully, as far as Elinor was concerned, her friend did not raise the subject of Luc Pascal once. When it was time for Catriona to go back to work, Elinor spent the days alone, happy to continue to enjoy Paris.

In spite of her enjoyment, Elinor knew she was simply putting off the day when she would have to return home and face the unpalatable truth that her career was still stalled with no sign of an upturn. She was enjoying her coffee one morning, her mind preoccupied by her professional woes, when the phone rang. Expecting it to be for Catriona, she spoke her name in a perfunctory way only to be surprised by Andrew's voice at the other end.

'Hi, Ellie, it's me, Andrew. Your father gave me your number. Hope you don't mind me calling.'

'Of course not. What can I do for you?'

'That's what I like, Ellie. Straight to the point. The thing is, Gerry is coming back to London. That knee of his is playing up and he thinks he's going to need an operation. Naturally that leaves us with no-one to cover that trade conference. Now, you've expressed an interest before and you are on the spot.'

'I'll take the assignment, Andrew,' she said without hesitation.

'That's great, Ellie. I've given Gerry your number and he's going to get in touch and fill you in before he leaves. I'll send your accreditation by express so you should be able to start your new post within a few days. Usual expenses apply but you know all about that. Good luck, Ellie.'

★ ★ ★

'Events really seem to be going quite slowly. Between you and me, Ellie, I'm not too heartbroken to be giving up this assignment.'

Gerry's expression was as doleful as his voice and Elinor's heart sank. When she had agreed to meet him at a café to be briefed before his return to London, she had expected to be given a resumé of the progress so far but, according to Gerry, there wasn't any.

'Or if there is,' he went on, 'the Press isn't being told about. I've never known a conference where the delegates are so tight-lipped. I blame that Luc Pascal.'

'Really, why is that?'

'Well, he seems to be running the show and he seems to exert an iron control over the delegates. They won't speak to us on or off the record and the daily Press briefings are so bland they're worse than useless.'

After attending several of the Press briefings, Elinor could see exactly what Gerry had been complaining about. Each one consisted of nothing more than banal statements which revealed little and even when some of the seasoned reporters she was working with asked incisive questions, they were stonewalled.

'I've never known a conference like it, honey,' a veteran female reporter from New York complained. 'Those guys in there could be discussing the outbreak of a new trade war and we wouldn't know about it.'

Elinor shared her frustration, and Gerry's comments about exploiting her connection with Luc Pascal crept into her mind once more. Later that evening she pulled her jeans out of the laundry basket and rescued Luc's card from the back pocket where it had remained since she had received it. She tapped it against the palm of her hand, her thoughts in a whirl. If Luc knew she was now covering the trade conference he might refuse to see her, but it would be totally unethical not to tell him at all.

Wondering how to handle the situation, she came up with a compromise. She would arrange to meet him and tell him the truth when they were face to face. That way she had a small chance of persuading him to speak to her on the record before he blew up! She dialled the number on the card before she could lose her nerve and the phone was answered instantly.

'Luc, it's Elinor here. I'm sorry I haven't been in touch earlier. The flowers were beautiful, thank you.'

'I'm glad you liked them,' he said crisply.

'The thing is, you mentioned dinner on the card and I wondered if the invitation was still open.'

Elinor had been aiming for a bright, flirtatious manner and, as silence greeted her words, she wondered nervously if she had put on a convincing display. Then his reply came.

'It would be delightful to see you, Elinor, and catch up on news. Tell me, how are you enjoying your assignment?'

She should have known she could not hide anything from Luc! Clearly he had noticed her name on the list of correspondents.

'Look, I'm not getting in touch just because of my new job,' she began defensively, to be greeted by a sceptical laugh.

'Really? Then you disappoint me. I was hoping you were intending to dazzle me with your beauty and steal all my professional secrets!'

Scarlet-faced, Elinor tried to extricate herself.

'This was obviously a bad idea. I'm sorry I troubled you.'

'No, wait! I would like to see you, but I'm not in Paris at the moment as I'm working at the family home. Could you come down this weekend? It's only a few hours' travelling time from Paris and I could send a car for you.'

'Of course that would be lovely.'

Had she really spoken those words? After Luc told her that someone would call and confirm what time she would be collected on Saturday morning, she replaced the receiver and sat in a daze. Why had she just agreed to spend the weekend with him after that teasing phone call? To be fair, she could hardly condemn Luc for baiting her when, to her shame, she had been all set to exploit their relationship for professional gain. That was now out of the question, so why accept his invitation?

Because she wanted to see him again! The renegade thought took her by surprise and she wondered, with an anticipatory shiver, what a weekend alone with Luc would mean for their relationship, and also what would it do for her emotional state which had been so volatile since facing rejection at the hands of his brother?

5

As the car rounded the bend, Elinor craned her neck to catch her first glimpse of Chateau Pascal. An avenue of lime trees led to a two-storeyed, white building, each tall, arched window flanked by green shutters, now open to welcome the mid-morning sun, window boxes of trailing pelargoniums in red and pinks providing a splash of colour and an air of informality to a classical French façade.

Luc appeared at the open doorway as soon as the car drew to a halt and, after greeting her, it was he, not the driver, who carried her small suitcase up the flight of steps and through the double doors into the hallway. As Luc dropped her suitcase at his feet Elinor's gaze swung around. Although the white pillars, rising to a decorative plaster-work ceiling, and the marbled floor, spoke of a much earlier age the panelled walls were painted cream, the pictures embellishing them were contemporary water-colours and the broad staircase which swept away from them to curve to the right was carpeted in a crisp mint green. She gave voice to her approval.

'It has a very light and airy feel to it, Luc. Quite modern, in fact.'

'I am glad you like it. I have made considerable effort in the last few years to rid the house of its museum look. My late father never wanted to change anything and as this house has been in my family since before the Revolution you can imagine what it used to look like.'

Elinor could not resist a mischievous question.

'And how did the Pascal family manage to retain their property during revolutionary times when so many others lost everything?'

Her query elicited a grim smile.

'It is not wise to delve too deeply into

the activities of my family during those turbulent times. Let us just say,' he added, as he drew her arm through his, 'that the Pascals can always be relied on for their resourcefulness.'

And nothing's changed there, she concluded to herself, certain that Luc Pascal would always find himself on the winning side.

Next moment they were stepping into the drawing-room and Elinor forgot all about distant Pascals as she exclaimed her delight. Sunlight poured through the open french doors on to the gleaming wooden floors, partially covered by Chinese silk rugs in blues and greys.

'I see this room has been subjected to your modernising touch,' she commented.

Luc surprised her by saying that his mother had refurbished the room some years before but, instead, of elaborating, he left, saying he would fetch a tray of coffee from the kitchen, leaving Elinor alone. She wandered across to the handsome fireplace, drawn to the two portraits in oil placed immediately above it. Close scrutiny confirmed what she suspected. She was looking at Monsieur and Madame Pascal. Now she knew why Luc and Jean Pierre differed so much in appearance. Luc, with the determined set of his chin and his dark colouring had the mark of his father about him whilst Jean Pierre had inherited the lighter complexion and softer features of his mother.

'My parents commissioned those paintings to celebrate their twenty-fifth wedding anniversary. Unfortunately their marriage did not last much longer.'

Elinor turned to find Luc unloading a tray on to a low table. She strolled across to collect her coffee from him, then, drinking from the exquisite porcelain cup, she eyed the portrait of Madame Pascal once more.

'Jean Pierre spoke little of his mother. Was there some sort of estrangement?'

'You could say that, Elinor. You see,

when she left the marriage she left us, too. I was already at university and able to cope but Jean Pierre, who was still only a teenager, was devastated.'

'Did you lose complete contact with your mother?'

'At first we did have some contact but it's difficult to retain links when you are in different countries. To be fair to my mother, I don't think the years of her marriage were easy for her. There was a large age gap between my parents and I don't believe she was ever truly at home as the chatelaine of Chateau Pascal. Consequently, when she fell in love with a fellow Texan she returned with him to her native state.'

As Elinor drank her coffee it occurred to her that she had learned more about the Pascal family in a few moments' conversation with Luc than she had learned from Jean Pierre in the whole of their courtship. During that time she had opened up to him completely, no area of her life hidden, but coming to Chateau Pascal was reminding her that Jean Pierre had not responded in kind. There had been an air of secrecy about him which, at the time, she had chosen to ignore, to her cost as it had turned out.

Rapt in her own thoughts Elinor didn't hear Luc's remark until it was repeated.

'If you've finished your coffee, perhaps you'd like to look around the house and grounds.'

'Of course.'

She replaced her cup on the tray and prepared to follow Luc out of the drawing-room.

Luc's renovation programme still had some way to go, she realised, as they wandered from room to room, as many of them still had the cluttered look and the stolid furniture of an earlier age but where Luc had made changes she could only approve of the way in which he had added more touches whilst respecting the original features. Their indoor tour concluded, they stepped out into the sunshine.

Luc stopped to open a small gate set into a closely-trimmed beech hedge, and led her through into a herb garden. They ended their tour at the stables and it was there Luc issued a challenge.

'You were brought up in the English countryside, Elinor, and I know every little girl in your village would have ridden from an early age.'

'As it happens, I do know how to ride, although I'm a little out of practice.'

'No matter,' Luc said breezily. 'We have a delightful mare, Rosemary, who will suit you beautifully. Come, we'll go back to the house now to have a light lunch and I will tell Jacques, our head groom, to have the horses saddled and ready for us to ride later.'

'And which one will you ride?' she asked.

'One of our new stallions, Rapide, newly arrived from Ireland.'

★　★　★

'She's delightful, Luc.'

With a neat head and a smooth action the dappled grey being walked up and down by Jacques looked like an ideal mount to Elinor. She wasn't so sure about Luc's choice and as the handsome bay flattened his ears and rolled his eyes on Luc's approach, she could only be thankful that she did not face a battle of wills with the temperamental thoroughbred.

To her surprise, instead of mounting straight away, Luc stroked down the muzzle of the horse with a gentle action and murmured to it, low-voiced, in French. Rapide tossed his head but already Elinor could see a change as his ears pricked up and, as Luc continued the gentle caress, his murmurings almost rhythmic, the horse stopped shifting from side to side until it was standing, its head slightly lowered in a gesture of submission.

Just as he was about to mount, Luc caught sight of Elinor's face. He leaned against Rapide's flank, arms folded across his broad chest and said, 'You look surprised, Elinor. Tell me, when I spoke of mastering Rapide, did you expect more macho methods?'

'Yes,' she admitted. 'I'd no doubt you'd impose your will on Rapide but I expected a less than subtle, gentle approach.'

He threw his head back and gave a great bark of laughter.

'I do not know whether to be flattered or insulted by your assessment of my character. But I will tell you one thing, Elinor. Sometimes it is the subtler approach which wins us prizes that may otherwise elude us for ever.'

He turned and swung himself up into the saddle.

Now what did he mean by that? Elinor was intrigued by the quixotic nature of the man who, in turn, antagonised her, mystified her and, to be honest, occasionally charmed her.

The route Luc had chosen led through woodland and Elinor was glad of the shade afforded by the trees and, also, of the tranquillity of the setting. She was almost sorry when Luc broke the companionable silence.

'We will come to some open land soon, Elinor. Let's give the horses their heads and enjoy their strength and speed.'

They matched action to words as soon as the countryside opened up before them, Rapide setting off first and Rosemary making a valiant effort to keep up. The gap between them soon widened but Elinor made no effort to urge Rosemary on, content only to enjoy the exhilaration of the gallop. In front of her Luc was beginning to slow his mount but, before she could gain on him, he veered to the right and disappeared.

She followed, only to find herself on a narrow track with Luc nowhere in sight. At the end of the track was a farm gate wide open and through it she could see Rapide, contentedly grazing. As Rosemary picked her way through, Luc came into view, sitting on top of a pile of felled trees, their trunks forming a natural seating area. After sliding off Rosemary she went to join him, pulling off her riding hat, happy to be free of its constraints.

She had drawn her hair back from her face and plaited it into one thick braid and as she seated herself next to Luc he commented, 'You look like a schoolgirl with your hair like that, Elinor, out for the day with the pony club.'

In a light-hearted gesture he went to lift up the braid but as his hand touched her bare skin, to her horror, she trembled.

'You don't have to flinch every time I come near you, Elinor,' he said.

'I'm not flinching,' she said tersely, disconcerted that she was speaking the truth and adding inwardly that his touch and his nearness were having quite the opposite effect.

In a moment of self-revelation, she knew that if he were to take her into his arms right now she would not pull back. The knowledge sent a mixture of emotions sweeping through her and she fought for her own inner control.

'It's been a lovely afternoon, Luc, but I guess we should be getting back now. This heat is rather tiring,' she suddenly blurted out.

'If you say so,' was Luc's brusque response and if she could have seen his face as he watched her retreating back she would have been unnerved by the dark-eyed fury of his gaze.

They were silent during their ride back and after they had handed over their mounts to Jacques and were making their way back to the house he surprised her by announcing that one of his neighbours was holding a reception that evening and that he had accepted for both of them. Relieved that she would not have to spend the evening alone with him Elinor expressed her approval but asked what sort of party it would be.

'Oh, Marianne has great style and elegance. Her parties are renowned for their good food and impressive guest lists. Invitations are sought after.'

His words conjured up an image of a sophisticated evening filled with the cream of the local society and Elinor was suddenly grateful that Catriona had insisted on her bringing a selection of dresses from her own collection.

Later that evening, as she nervously slipped on a dress in front of the cheval mirror, unable to decide between two gowns, she fervently wished her friend was there with her, and not only to advise on fashion matters. Suddenly indifferent to what she was going to wear she slumped down on the bed, her thoughts crowding in on her as she focused once more on what had happened earlier between herself and Luc. An innocent moment, a simple gesture had resulted in a tension between them so palpable that if she had not walked away right then she would have done something she would have regretted. She might even have instigated it!

That one brief kiss in Luc's hotel room had provided ample warning that Luc exercised a potent attraction for her. She had found it within herself to resist then so why had she put herself in danger once more by coming to Chateau Pascal? And what of Jean Pierre? She tried to conjure up her ex-fiancé's face. She failed, tried again, and was confronted with the disturbing image of eyes that were sinfully dark gazing back at her as though they could pierce her very soul. She jumped up and began to pace about, shocked at how profoundly Luc Pascal seemed to fill her thoughts.

Relations between herself and Luc had always been fraught because, quite simply, she had blamed him for the breakdown of her relationship with his brother. But, in the absence of any reason that had made real sense, hadn't she simply looked for a scapegoat? Venting her anger on Luc, she admitted candidly for the first time, had hardly been fair.

The house phone rang, puncturing her thoughts, and when she picked it up it was Luc.

'The car will be here in twenty minutes, Elinor. I will see you downstairs.'

He cut off before she could reply and Elinor seized the nearest dress which had been flung on to the bed and pulled it on. It was an off-the-shoulder, slim-fitting gown in black satin, immaculately cut by Catriona in classic style. She had already put her hair up, and had only to add some pearl ear studs and a single string of pearls.

Did she look a little conventional for the fashionable crowd she would have to mix with, she wondered. For one panic-stricken moment she decided she would never be able to match Luc for style and glamour. A crazy desire to pack up and leave was flitting through her head when a sharp rap at the door caused her to start.

'Come in,' she called out tentatively.

Luc's tall figure was framed in the

doorway, in black dinner suit, the white, silk, pleated shirt in sharp contrast to the tanned face. His dark eyes were unreadable as he took in her appearance.

'I'm not sure this dress is suitable,' she said hesitantly.

Elinor's voice trailed away as it occurred to her that she sounded just like some gauche teenager. Her social skills had deserted her even before the evening had begun, she thought.

'It depends on what you mean by suitable,' he said. 'It isn't yet illegal to set a man's pulse racing, but perhaps it ought to be!'

Elinor took that as a compliment, and with her spirits suddenly soaring, she collected her handbag and prepared to join Luc.

6

On their journey there Elinor learned that their hostess, Marianne Dubois, was a businesswoman involved in the export of antiques who had bought the estate adjoining Chateau Pascal some ten years before. This brief biography hardly prepared Elinor for the tall figure greeting guests in the hallway of one of the most stylish houses in the area.

Elinor estimated Marianne to be in her mid-thirties and, like many women of that age, at the height of her beauty. A little light make-up was all that was needed to emphasise the strong, well-defined features. Her figure was stunning and shown off to best advantage in a figure-hugging dress in silver-grey lace with a square, low-cut bodice. On seeing them she held out her honey-toned arms to Luc. A volley of French words followed as she kissed him on each cheek. Standing at their side, and wishing fervently that she could be elsewhere, Elinor was just about to slip away when Marianne released Luc, who looked far too pleased with himself, Elinor decided sourly. Marianne turned towards her.

'Mademoiselle, enchanté.'

Elinor took the hand offered and responded in French. Although she was fluent she knew her accent left a lot to be desired but her self-confidence was not helped when Marianne spoke in perfect English.

'I see you are still learning our language, mademoiselle. No matter. Many of my business associates here tonight are from English-speaking countries. I am sure you will find someone to talk to.'

Linking arms, she and Luc wandered off, leaving Elinor alone, looking with fury at their retreating backs. She didn't know with whom to be angrier, Luc or Marianne. It was Marianne who had patronised her but Luc was her escort and he had strolled off with their hostess to have a cosy tête-à-tête, whilst she was left on her own!

Looking round her uncertainly she was relieved when a member of staff, in dark blue livery, approached to inform her that the oyster and champagne buffet was in one of the reception rooms on her left. Thanking him she went through and joined the small throng of people already there. Elinor, realising she couldn't just stand and eat all night, attempted to start a conversation with a couple next to her. Unfortunately, she could not understand their broad, regional accent and found herself nodding her head a good deal in what she hoped were appropriate places.

At last she managed a tactful withdrawal and, as she followed a crowd of people from the supper room into what appeared to be a ballroom, she decided that, if the evening continued in the same disastrous vein, she would simply cut it short and walk back to the chateau. Just then a young man with an untidy mop of fair hair brushed against her, managing to tread on her foot. Stepping back abruptly, dismay written all over his face, he attempted to apologise in French with a distinctly American accent.

'It's quite all right,' she cut in before he had a chance to mangle the language further. 'I've already managed to demolish a few toes myself!'

His expression turned to one of relief.

'You speak English!'

'Since I was two years old,' Elinor countered, and they both laughed.

After introducing themselves it quickly became apparent that Terry Stevens was feeling as out of place as she was.

'I hardly know Marianne,' he confided, 'but we've done some useful business together and when she asked me to this reception I thought it would be diplomatic to attend. What about you, Elinor? How do you come to know her?'

'I don't know her at all,' Elinor confessed. 'I'm staying at Chateau Pascal, the neighbouring estate, and was brought here by my host. Apart from Luc I don't know a soul.'

'And where is the guy who brought you?'

'A good question,' Elinor answered drily. 'He was monopolised by our hostess as soon as we arrived and I haven't seen him since!'

Terry brushed one hand through his unruly blonde hair, shooting her an uncertain glance.

'In that case, would you mind if I asked you to dance?'

'I would be delighted to dance with you,' Elinor said, charmed by his diffident manner.

Terry proved himself an adept dancer and Elinor, who loved to dance, threw caution to the winds as she moved fluently to the rapid rhythms, casting aside, for the moment, her annoyance at being dumped by her escort as soon as the glamorous Marianne had appeared. After several energetic dances they decided to sit one out and Elinor commandeered a side table whilst Terry went to fetch her a glass of champagne.

'I'm on mineral water as I'm driving,' he told her ruefully, slipping into the seat beside her, 'but it won't stop me enjoying your company. Cheers.'

Elinor responded by raising her glass to his, and they began to chat. Terry proved good company, as interested in what she had to say as in his own conversation, and gradually Elinor was able to piece together a biography in which a youthful passion for antiques, especially for pre-Revolutionary French pieces, had led eventually to a thriving import business.

Not even Terry's lively chatter could hold Elinor's interest, though, when her eyes strayed on to the dance floor and pinpointed, amongst the crowd, Luc and Marianne. Her arms were wound round his neck, her dark head raised to his.

Elinor threw her head back to drink the rest of her champagne in one go, gave a laugh which sounded forced even to her own ears, and interrupted Terry in mid flow to suggest they should re-join the dancers. Once on the dance floor, she pulled Terry close as they swayed to the slower rhythms of the music, her eyes closing as she rested her head on his shoulder. She let out a contented sigh but even as she did so something jarred deep in her subconscious.

Reluctant to respond, she pulled Terry closer but the unsettling feeling continued and, eventually, her eyes opened lazily to find herself looking over Terry's shoulder. Marianne and Luc were only a few feet away. Marianne was nestled in his arms, but Luc's eyes were not on his partner. They were on her, and they were fixing her with a look of such intense dislike that, instantly, Elinor recoiled.

'Hey, are you all right?'

Terry gave her a solicitous look.

'I'm just rather hot. Perhaps we could sit the next one out.'

'I've got a better suggestion,' Terry said, as they turned to leave the dance floor. 'I don't know about you, Elinor, but those oysters didn't really satisfy my appetite. I'm staying at a really great hotel and the lady who runs it is always happy to lay on late-night suppers. What do you say? Would you like to join me in a meal? I'll drive you back to where you're staying afterwards,' he cajoled, as she failed to respond.

As she glanced around, unsure of what to do, a gap appeared in the crowd of dancers and, briefly, she caught sight of Luc, still entwined with Marianne in an embrace which spoke volumes about their true relationship.

'Let's go,' she said, taking a surprised Terry by the hand.

If Elinor had any qualms, after her Paris experience with Jake, about dining with a man she had just met, they were soon dispelled when, after settling down to a delicious supper rustled up by the smiling hotelier, Terry proceeded to bring out photographs of members of his family and regaled her with tales of the small Californian town in which he had grown up.

'What about you, Elinor? Do you come from a small town?'

'It doesn't even warrant the name town,' Elinor confessed, explaining that West Hope consisted of a huddle of houses, a church, pub, shop and duck pond! 'Nor are there any ducks. They flew away to join a larger colony on a lake nearby!'

They laughed and then the conversation flowed as they discussed their respective professions until Elinor caught sight of a clock in the hallway.

'Terry, it's past one! I really must go.'

Terry fished in his trouser pocket for his keys.

'It'll only take about five minutes to get you back. No need to worry.'

Terry was as good as his word and, a

few moments later, he was drawing up outside Chateau Pascal.

She reached across to kiss him on the cheek.

'Good-night, Terry, and thank you so much for a pleasant evening.'

'Glad to be of service. I was at a loose end before you showed up.'

They parted with a smile and, as Elinor made her way up the flight of steps which led to the double doors, she wondered why she and Luc had never been able to establish the sort of easy rapport which she had just experienced with a virtual stranger. It was only when she reached the door that it occurred to her, for the very first time that, as Luc was not with her, she had no means of getting in. Louis, the houseman, would have retired to bed long since, and would be incensed if she woke him at this late hour.

As she stood, hesitating, the door suddenly swung back to reveal the tall figure of Luc framed in the doorway. The light was behind him, leaving his face in darkness, but the tension emanating from him was clear to see.

'I see you're back,' Elinor began but her words were cut short when he flung away from her, growling, 'In here.'

Elinor had little choice but to follow him into the library but as soon as they were inside she rounded on him.

'I don't know why you're behaving in this churlish way, Luc, but I'm not the sort of woman to be impressed by these high-handed tactics! Have you nothing to say for yourself?' Elinor rapped.

'I am just trying to find the right words, only I find your prim and proper manner a little hard to take since you seem to have no qualms about leaving a party with a man you have just met. It seems to be quite a speciality of yours, come to think of it.'

His sneering insinuation was breathtaking in its hypocrisy, coming from a man who had spent the entire evening wrapped around a beautiful woman!

'You may have escorted me to the soirée tonight,' she snapped, 'but once there it was obvious that your attentions would be otherwise engaged. It's hardly surprising I looked for more congenial company. And you have no right to imply I was doing anything wrong!'

'No right! Clearly I have no rights at all where you are concerned whereas any callow youth who takes your fancy — '

'Luc, just listen a moment, please!'

Suddenly Elinor was tired of this crazy conversation and eager for a way out of the impasse she and Luc were busily creating.

Drawing a deep breath, she said, 'I don't know what you've been thinking but I've spent the last few hours with a perfectly sweet young man who spent most of the time showing me his family photographs.'

Luc brushed one hand through his hair distractedly, then half turned away, muttering in French. Then he rounded on her.

'I swear, Elinor, that you will turn me into a crazy man! Why did you disappear with this young man without leaving a message?'

'To pay you back, of course! As soon as we got to the reception you disappeared with the hostess and I was left kicking my heels. I knew no one, I felt ill-at-ease, so when I bumped into a charming American I was happy to spend time with him. I admit my behaviour was a little petulant but I hardly think it warrants an accusation I'm some sort of scarlet woman!'

Luc, his head in his hands during her tirade, now raised it and the bleak expression on his face caused her flow of words to come to a halt. She waited expectantly but when he spoke it was barely audible.

'I am sorry, Elinor. My only excuse is that I do not believe I have had one moment's rational thought since I saw you for the very first time.'

But the first time he had seen her she had been his brother's fiancée! Thinking she must have misunderstood, she remained silent as he went on.

'As for this evening, again I am sorry if I appeared to neglect you. It was not intentional. I extricated myself from Marianne as soon as I could and came in search of you. Unfortunately, you had already found solace elsewhere.'

'It really isn't any business of mine whom you spend your time with, Luc. Marianne is very beautiful, and clearly you have much in common. I expect you're very happy together.'

'All that you say is true, except Marianne and I are not involved as you seem to be implying.'

'I've just said, it's none of my business.'

'I'm afraid it is.'

His eyes held her in thrall as he went on.

'Elinor, this is something I hoped I would never have to reveal, but things have become too complicated between us. Marianne is in love with Jean Pierre. Those two have been involved, on and off, for years.'

'No!'

Even as she flung the word out, she knew the truth of what he was saying. She had seen the thinly-veiled hostility in the older woman's eyes, but she wanted to hit back, to assuage some of the pain that was seeping through her.

'You're just saying that because you want to humiliate me. You never thought I was good enough to join your precious family and you put every obstacle in the way of my marriage to your brother, didn't you?'

'No, I did not.'

A look of fury flashed across his face and she took a step backwards as he came towards her.

'What do you want me to say, Elinor, that the thought of your marriage to my brother was repugnant to me?'

He caught hold of her, shaking her slightly as he went on, his voice tight as though each word was being torn from him.

'Because that is the truth. You see, I did not want you to become Jean Pierre's wife because I had fallen in love with you myself!'

Elinor looked up at him, aghast, then, with a downward thrust of her elbows she was free and, twisting away from him, she fled. She had no thought other than to seek the sanctuary of her room and when she had reached it her next thought was that she must leave Chateau Pascal immediately! Throwing open her case she began to pile in things which she had only just unpacked that very morning until the futility of the venture struck her and she sat down on the bed and burst into tears.

She had barely acknowledged a knock at the door when he entered.

'Elinor, we have to talk.'

He seated himself next to her, turning towards her.

'You must believe me when I say that I had no intention of blurting out my feelings in such away. Everything just got so crazy.'

In a small voice Elinor said, 'Just tell me everything, from the beginning.'

He looked down at his hands.

'I was concerned when Jean Pierre announced his engagement. We had never met you, he had not known you for long and, although he denied it, I believed him to be still involved with Marianne. I went to England full of trepidation, fearful that my rather feckless brother had got himself involved in an entanglement he would regret. But when I met you, let's just say that my reaction was not one that a man should have towards his intended sister-in-law! From that moment I ceased to oppose the marriage, fearful that I would be motivated, not out of concern for my brother's welfare, but for my own selfish reasons! I was in an agony, Elinor. I distanced myself from you both and awaited the inevitable outcome.'

He let out a heavy sigh, then continued.

'All seemed to be going well between you two and then the night before the wedding Jean Pierre received a phone call from Marianne. I have no idea what the call was about but they spoke at length and, after that, Jean Pierre was very agitated. He told me he could not marry you but refused to say why. I can surmise that it was something to do with his relationship with Marianne, but, to this day I do not know the real reason for his actions.'

For the first time, he looked her fully in the face.

'In that, I told you the truth, but what I did not reveal was my relief at his news. Then, when I was faced with the pain my treacherous brother had caused you I felt terribly guilty that I had been pleased by his decision!'

Experiencing a mixture of emotions Elinor tried to put some of her thoughts into words.

'But why didn't you, at least, tell me about Marianne? Why did you allow me to blame you for my broken romance?'

'It was Jean Pierre who should have confessed everything to you, but my charming brother had disappeared, leaving others to pick up the pieces.'

'But I took out all my anger and frustration on you,' Elinor persisted. 'And you made little effort to defend yourself.'

'Be fair, Elinor, you were in no mood to listen! Besides, seeing the contempt in your eyes as you looked at me brought me back down to earth. Ever since Jean Pierre had told me of his decision I had entertained a crazy notion that, one day, I might be able to replace him in your affections. When I faced you in your house that morning and saw the misery my brother had caused I realised that you would not want anything to do with anyone named Pascal, ever again. My decision to grant you an interview was an attempt to help you piece your career back together. I had no real hope that it would improve relations between us and so it proved. When we parted in London I resigned myself to the fact that I would not see you again.'

'And yet fate brought us back together.'

'A cruel fate, Elinor. The resentment towards me was still there but this time I decided I would try some old-fashioned courtship and this weekend at my family home was to be a start. I intended to show you a different side of me, Elinor, to charm you into my heart but as is often the way when I am around you, things got a little out of hand.'

In a moment of brutal self-honesty Elinor realised that, right from the beginning, she had sensed that Luc had some sort of interest in her and, on her part, there had been an answering pull. Reading the emotions on her face Luc was quick to exploit her uncertainty.

'Perhaps you need a little help in clarifying your thoughts.'

His dark eyes tantalised her as his lips moved against her soft mouth in a gentle caress and Elinor responded, her fingers winding into the silky strands of his hair as the kiss deepened. She felt as though she was floating in a dream.

Next moment, an insistent noise had Luc pulling away with a groan of resignation and Elinor watched in dismay as he reached to one side to pick up the phone. When he finished the conversation abruptly and turned to her the expression on his face said it all.

'A delegation is threatening to walk out. The talks are in crisis. I have to go, Elinor.'

Trying to keep the disappointment out of her voice, she said, 'Of course you must go, Luc.'

He stood up and then took both her hands in his.

'You will never know how hard it is to leave you right now.'

'I know that.'

Elinor looked up at him with moistened eyes, adding shyly, 'There will be another time, Luc.'

'And soon, ma chère. Wait here for me. I will call you tomorrow.'

She nodded her assent and then the door was closing behind him.

7

Elinor woke with a start, and, as memories of what had happened the day before flooded into her mind, her head fell back on to the pillow. It was all too much to take in. She had arrived at Chateau Pascal with some vaguely-formed plan of improving relations with Luc only to find herself, at the end of one extraordinary day, in his arms.

Bewildered by the turn of events and the speed with which her relationship with Luc seemed to be developing, she wondered about the wisdom of staying at Chateau Pascal as he had requested. Wouldn't it be better to return to Paris and give herself time to discover her true feelings without the distraction of Luc's presence?

As she pondered her dilemma, she found herself re-living the moment when Luc had held her in his arms and, recalling the look in his eyes, she knew she must stay and face up to what had happened between them. Having come to some sort of resolution, she threw back the bed clothes and climbed out of bed, the feeling persisting within her that today might well determine the direction her future life would take.

When she went in search of Louis, the houseman, to tell him of Luc's unexpected departure in the middle of the night, he took it in his stride, giving her the impression that he had long since ceased to be surprised by his master's erratic lifestyle. He busied himself making fresh coffee for Elinor and after she had drunk her fill, and demolished a fresh croissant, she wandered outside to take in the morning air.

Elinor decided to go for a walk before the heat of the day closed in, and after collecting her sun hat from her room, she set off, relishing the early-morning freshness. She went farther than intended, became slightly lost, and then, after asking directions from a fellow walker made her way back to the house, reaching it just before midday.

After a light lunch on the terrace she decided to check out the books in the library, intent on a lazy afternoon, and was just passing through the hallway when the telephone rang. It was Luc, and she could tell immediately from the formal way he greeted her that he was not alone.

'Elinor, good morning. I wonder if you could do me a very great favour?'

'Of course. What do you wish me to do?'

'A courier has been despatched to the house and should be with you shortly. I need you to give him certain documents from the library safe.'

He proceeded to tell her how to locate the safe and which documents he wanted, finishing on a warning note.

'I will give you the combination of the safe now. Please make sure you destroy the paper you write it on as soon as you have completed the task as

131

no-one else must have access.'

He lowered his voice to dictate the ten-digit number and Elinor wrote it on the notepad on the table.

'I know I can rely on you. Au revoir, ma chère,' he ended.

Picking up the notepad she hurried to the library. Following Luc's instructions she ran her fingers up the spine of a leather-bound book which jutted out of the middle shelf to the left of the chimney breast, grasped it, and then pulled it towards her. There was a clicking sound and then she carried on tugging as several of the false book-shelves swung out. Behind them was a solid, old-fashioned safe and, holding the notepad in one hand, she dialled the combination. To her relief there was a click and she was able to pull the door open and peer into an aperture filled to the brim with folders.

She stacked the dossiers required on the coffee table, closed the safe and shelves behind her and then tore the sheet of paper with the combination number on it into tiny pieces before disposing of them in the waste-paper basket.

Sitting down, she decided to remain with the documents until the courier arrived and was just wondering vaguely whether all the books on the shelves were false or whether she might be able to find one to while away these idle moments when the door bell chimed, to be followed by the sound of Louis' footsteps across the hallway. Hurrying to the door, she opened it to find Louis engaged in conversation with a des-patch rider clad in black leather his helmet in one hand, a tan valise in the other. As she approached, Louis spoke in his broken English.

'The man, he is here, Monsieur Pascal send.'

Elinor checked the identity card the courier was holding out for her and then gestured for him to follow. Once in the library she handed over the documents; saw them packed safely into the valise, then after a brief thank you the man turned smartly on his heels and was gone.

Suddenly realising she had been gazing out of the window for the last few minutes dreaming of being with Luc once more, like a lovestruck teenager, she reminded herself that she couldn't spend the rest of her life lost in thought whenever Luc was absent. She went up to her room to write a letter to her father. After that, she settled herself on the terrace with a book but Luc's face rose up persistently between her and the page and she ended up flinging the book down in a fit of exasperation as she wondered, for the umpteenth time, when he would return.

When her straying eyes came to rest on the shutters belonging to the floor-length doors leading to the library, something niggled at the back of her mind. Surely Louis had said he would close all the shutters before he went out. Yet these shutters were wide open, leaving the hot afternoon sun to pour into the room. Somehow she couldn't imagine the efficient Louis forgetting something as routine as that. Who had opened them and why?

The answer snapped back at her. As the shutters and doors operated on simple locks, it would have been easy for any intruder to wrench them open whilst she was upstairs and help themselves to some of the exquisite objects on display! She leaped to her feet and hurried up to the library doors without stopping to think. They were half-open and she could see a figure in the far corner, shrouded in darkness, bending over something.

She stepped inside, her thoughts racing as she desperately tried to formulate the correct words in French, determined that when she did challenge him her voice would not tremble. She thought she was moving with the utmost care but some sixth sense must have alerted the man, for as she took another step into the room, he whipped round to face her. She froze. It was Jean Pierre!

For weeks after his betrayal, as she had wept into her pillow, she had fantasised about being face to face with him, having imaginary conversations in which he explained how it had all been a terrible mistake and if only she would forgive him they would resume their romance. Now she looked at him with no love in her heart, knowing that from the first moment they had met he had been betraying her with another woman, that their marriage would have been a disaster and his rejection of her at the last moment the greatest gift he could have bestowed on her.

As shock on Jean Pierre's face gave way to wariness, she found her voice at last.

'What are you doing here, Jean Pierre?'

'I could say the same to you. This is the last place I would expect to find you, Ellie.'

The diminutive, used by her father and old friends jarred. If he was trying to presume on past intimacy he was in for a big disappointment.

'I'm here at the invitation of Luc.'

Something flashed in the depths of his hazel eyes.

'He didn't wait long, did he? I noticed the way he used to look at you! Were you two cheating on me whilst you and I were together?'

Elinor gasped at the cheek of the man.

'Of course not! Only one person was cheating in our relationship!'

He flushed, his eyes shifting from hers.

'What has my sanctimonious brother been saying about me?'

'Only the truth, that you had a long-standing relationship with Marianne Dubois, one you conveniently forgot to tell me about.'

There was a silence and as Elinor watched different emotions play across his face her first, cynical thought was that he was frantically working out a cover story. Her next was to wonder what on earth she had ever seen in him. What she had once thought of a boyish charm she could now see was immaturity. As though he realised his power over her was finally broken, and evasion was no longer an option, he gave a shrug of indifference.

'Marianne is a mature woman. She knew I was not offering her anything permanent. She could live with that.'

'Even when you were planning to marry me?'

'Don't sound so shocked. It's been done before.'

The callous indifference of his tone momentarily robbed Elinor of her response. Staring at him wide-eyed, the expression on her face said it all and, his face twisting into a mocking smile, he concluded, 'It's just as well the marriage never took place, isn't it, Ellie?'

'Leaving me at the altar was probably the finest thing you've done in your life,' Elinor said with feeling.

'On that sour note, my dear, I think you and I should part.'

As he bent over his task once more,

she could see that he was intent on zipping up a small, bulging suitcase and, as he picked it up and swung around, Elinor took a step towards him.

'Hold on a minute, Jean Pierre. You never did tell me what you were doing here.'

'This is my family home. I don't have to explain my presence here to you,' was his sharp-tongued response.

'True, but why did you choose Louis' afternoon off when you would expect to find the place empty, and more to the point, why break in?'

She jerked her head in the direction of the open doors, the broken catch clearly visible. Jean Pierre's veneer of self control seemed to snap all of a sudden and he came closer, his face jutting into hers.

'I had to break into my own family home because my dear brother has changed all the locks and has forbidden Louis to let me in. He wants to keep everything for himself, you see. Well, he's welcome to this mausoleum but there are things here that belong to me, and I've taken them.'

It was only then that Elinor noticed that several porcelain figurines were missing from the mantelpiece.

'Just cashing in early on my trust fund.'

He went to brush past her and as Elinor tried to detain him with a hand on his arm he turned and pushed her with such force that she staggered back, falling against the side of a carver chair, the wooden edges of the arm digging sharply into the small of her back so that pain shot through her, dizzying her senses.

Without a backward glance Jean Pierre disappeared through the french windows leaving Elinor to slump into the chair, her head in her hands as she tried to steady herself, disappointment sweeping through her at her failure to prevent Jean Pierre from stealing from Luc. Next moment as she stood up and pain shot up her spine, all thought of the lost treasures went out of her mind as she realised she might have damaged her back. Walking stiffly to the doors, she closed them and then went up to her room.

There, she pulled off her dress and, organising the cheval mirror so that she could see her back, she was able to take a good look at the weal at the base of her spine which was rapidly turning purple. There was a first aid box in her room and she was able to place some soothing balm on the injured area. Reassured that the abrasion was fairly superficial she lay down on the bed, intent on taking a short rest. The emotional turmoil of her encounter with Jean Pierre had taken its toll, however, and when her eyelids began to droop she found herself unable to resist, quickly falling into a deep sleep.

She woke with a start and knew, instinctively, that she was not alone in the house and, as Louis was not due back until the evening, it must mean that Jean Pierre had returned! She leaped out of bed, pulling on her dress as she made for the door, her bruised back forgotten, determined that this time Jean Pierre would not find it so easy to walk out of Chateau Pascal with possessions he was not entitled to.

Wanting to take him by surprise, she tiptoed downstairs in her bare feet, crossed the hallway and then paused outside the closed door of the library. Something stirred. Taking a deep breath she flung the door open, to come face to face with Luc. He was standing in the centre of the room and she wanted to run to him, but something on his face stopped her.

As she hesitated, he said dully, 'I would have thought you would have gone by now.'

What did he mean?

'But I promised to stay until your return. But never mind that,' she added impatiently. 'Jean Pierre has been here!'

'Of course, he has. His handiwork is everywhere.'

'I'm afraid he's taken some porcelain.

I tried to stop him but it was no use. I'm so sorry.'

He was looking at her as though her words had barely registered.

'What do a few figurines matter? The dossiers Jean Pierre has stolen could put all our negotiations at risk if they fall into the wrong hands.'

Now Elinor noticed the open safe and, as the significance sank in, she repeated in a shocked voice, 'He's stolen files?'

It was as though something snapped within Luc.

'Do not look at me with those big eyes! Do not presume on my self control lasting! I am trying not to be too hard on you, Elinor. I know how persuasive my brother can be, and when you love someone . . . '

'No! Listen to me, Luc! I did not help Jean Pierre. I discovered him just as he was leaving. I tried to stop him but he was too strong for me.'

'If you did not help him, Elinor, how did he get into the safe?'

143

'He used to live here,' Elinor responded wildly. 'He would know the combination.'

'No! I change the combination all the time and the current one was known only to myself and, from today, you. Explain to me how Jean Pierre could open the safe without your help.'

Elinor's eyes fell from his.

'I can't. You'll just have to accept my word that I did not help him.'

He stepped back from her as though he needed to increase the physical distance between them and as she waited she could see his inner turmoil reflected on his face. One hand brushed jerkily through his dark locks, his eyes closed briefly and when he spoke it was as though each word was wrenched from him.

'I wonder if I did a very selfish thing in trying to make you love me, for I can see now where your heart truly lies.'

Elinor wanted to cry out, to deny his assumption but, somehow, she could not find her voice. She started as he slammed the safe door shut and when he turned to her, his voice was devoid of all emotion.

'I cannot let this stand, Elinor, in spite of your involvement, but I will give you and Jean Pierre some time. I can conceal the loss of these documents for a little while but my patience will not last for ever.'

He picked up his jacket from the side of a chair.

'I have to return to the conference now but I will expect you to return everything within ten days or else the authorities will be informed. If you love Jean Pierre, persuade him to co-operate.'

At last she found her voice.

'I don't love Jean Pierre! I love you!'

But the sound of the door slamming shut drowned out her cry and she found herself pouring out her heart to an empty room.

8

The concièrge raised her eyebrows and waved one hand in graphic illustration of her point. Elinor nodded her head vigorously, fired another question and when her response was a shrug turned to Catriona with a sigh.

'It's just as we thought. Jean Pierre gave up his apartment some months ago, without leaving a forwarding address.'

Turning back to the concièrge she thanked her for her help and then took her friend's arm.

'Come on, let's go and get a coffee and think through what to do next.'

Seated at a corner table in an almost empty café Elinor stared gloomily at her frothy coffee. It was left to Catriona to break the silence.

'Look, Ellie, you're not responsible for the loss of the documents so why are you knocking yourself out trying to find Jean Pierre?'

'Those papers need returning, Cat. They contain sensitive information and in the wrong hands it could cause all sorts of trouble.'

'That's very public-spirited of you, and I know you're sincere, but that's not the only reason, is it?'

'No,' Elinor admitted tersely, stirring her coffee vigorously. 'I want to find out exactly how Jean Pierre got into that safe so I can clear myself.'

'Luc had no right to doubt you on such thin evidence! Why, he didn't even listen to your side of the story!'

'I was so shocked by it all I didn't put up much of a defence but even if I had, I don't think it would have made much difference. Nothing had been really resolved between Luc and me, you see. I was still trying to untangle my emotions. Part of me was terribly drawn to him but part of me was still holding back. I've no doubt Luc sensed that and, most likely, suspected that I was still in love with his brother. When it looked as though I'd helped Jean Pierre it must have seemed as though I'd confirmed his worst fears.'

'I think you're being a little too easy on the guy. Luc's behaviour sounded downright arrogant to me.'

'Oh, it was. Humility is not one of Luc's strong points. That's why we've spent most of our time together quarrelling!'

Elinor smiled for the first time since she had entered the coffee shop.

'What now, Ellie? Where do you go from here?' Catriona asked.

'There's only one other person I can turn to. Marianne Dubois. She's probably the only person who knows where Jean Pierre is.'

* * *

Marianne's home, seen in daylight for the first time by Elinor, brought a gasp of admiration to her lips as well as a matching comment from Catriona.

'What an extraordinary house!'

They had stopped the car just as they had rounded the bend in the driveway, giving them a perfect view of Chateau Dubois. Most of the blue-painted shutters were closed against the fierce morning sun, giving it a sleepy, domestic air at odds with its fort-like appearance.

'I just hope she's in,' Elinor said anxiously.

'Oh, we've done our homework,' Catriona said breezily. 'According to the staff at her Parisian shop she spends every Friday morning at home doing her accounts.'

'Then let's hope she tells her staff the truth!'

'In that case it's no use sitting here, is it? The sooner you and Marianne start talking, the better you'll feel.'

As usual she was right. Elinor climbed out with a resigned air and set off down the driveway, Catriona's words of farewell wafting along behind her.

'Don't forget, if you need any help, just yell.'

Turning briefly, she flashed her a smile of acknowledgement, glad now that she had agreed to Catriona driving her there. In spite of the reassurance her friend's presence brought, though, she could feel her stomach muscles knotting with apprehension as she approached the door and wondered, once more, what sort of reception she would receive.

A surprisingly modern touch was the intercom to the right of the door, Elinor thought, and after she pressed the buzzer she was surprised when Marianne herself answered with a terse, 'Bonjour.'

Knowing she spoke the language perfectly Elinor answered in English.

'This is Elinor Dale. I need to speak to you urgently, about Jean Pierre.'

She waited patiently, willing the woman on the other end to admit her and when, without another word, the door suddenly whirred open and she stood on the threshold, hesitating a little, before stepping inside.

Marianne was standing in the hallway and, at the sight of Elinor, she tilted her head to the right.

'In here, please.'

Elinor found herself in a delightful morning-room at the back of the house, half-open shutters spilling sun on to a wooden floor with a herringbone pattern, a rug in deep blue providing the only colour in a room dominated by seating in cream leather with muslin drapes at the window.

'Say what you have to say, mademoiselle. I have no time or patience for any nonsense,' Marianne said coldly.

Elinor could well believe it and, grateful for her plea for frank dealing, said, 'It's imperative I find Jean Pierre as soon as possible.'

'Why is that, may I ask?'

'Because he is a liar and a cheat. I can't tell you the full details as the situation's very sensitive.'

Marianne turned away abruptly, as

though afraid of revealing too much and, sitting down on one of the couches, gestured for her to follow suit.

'Please, mademoiselle, sit down.'

Although she still had the autocratic tones of a chatelaine talking to a recalcitrant member of staff, Elinor couldn't help feeling that her indignant outburst had changed something between them. As she settled herself opposite her hostess she took a gamble on what that might be.

'Did you think that I wanted to find Jean Pierre to re-kindle our romance?' she ventured.

'That did occur to me when you turned up on my doorstep just now.'

She was silent for a moment, frowning as though contemplating some inner conflict and then she burst out with, 'I hated you, did you know that?'

Elinor, realising that no reply was really necessary, remained silent as Marianne went on.

'You sec, in spite of my arrangement

with Jean Pierre, one that suited him far more than it did me, I had hoped that one day he would commit himself to me. Then you came along. You were fresh-faced, quite the ingénue, in fact, and, more to the point, closer to him in age than I was. And he offered you what he had never offered me — marriage, a future.'

Elinor felt she had to defend her rôle in the triangle.

'Look,' she said, 'I had no idea he was involved with anyone else. He never said a word to me about you.'

Marianne's face twisted into a bitter smile.

'And when I challenged him on his intentions towards you he insisted you were a mere diversion! It was Luc who told me of his wedding plans.'

Jean Pierre's audacity brought a gasp to Elinor's lips.

'His behaviour was even worse than I'd thought!'

'Oh, double-dealing has been second nature to Jean Pierre for a long time. It is astonishing to me that I . . . that I still . . . '

'Care for him?' Elinor suggested.

Marianne gave her head a sudden shake.

'I am an idiot, am I not? But we cannot always choose where we place our hearts.'

No, indeed, Elinor agreed silently, thinking of her fraught relationship with Luc. She was now feeling much more sympathetically disposed towards Marianne and offered a suggestion.

'I know Jean Pierre behaved abominably towards you but, in the end, he didn't marry me, did he? The conversation you had with him on the night before our wedding must have brought home to him what he would lose if he let you go.'

To her consternation Marianne threw back her head and laughed.

'My dear Elinor,' she said at last, 'Jean Pierre did not desert you for love of me! It was to save his own skin. I had alerted him, you see, to the fact that one of his scams had gone wrong. Over the years he had borrowed heavily on the strength of his expectations as everyone in the world of finance knew the Pascal inheritance would be a large one. Unfortunately for Jean Pierre, his father was all too well aware of his reckless nature and on his death he found out that Luc had inherited the house and estate whilst his own share of the fortune, including shares in the family business, had been put into a trust. He received a sizeable income each year but could not touch the capital.'

She paused a moment, leaving Elinor time to ask herself once more why she had allowed herself to be swept off her feet by a man she had known so little about. Resuming abruptly, Marianne elaborated further.

'Jean Pierre could only put off his creditors for so long and he began looking around for another source of income, and he found it in the family business. You see, for some years now, the Pascals have been diversifying their business interests and moving into leisure, retail, communications. Anyway, it was all getting a little complex and, after the death of their father, Luc gave Jean Pierre the task of assessing their operations with the view to slimming it down. I suspect it was an attempt to pacify his brother after the shock of his disinheritance.'

Marianne gave a typically Gallic shrug.

'Unfortunately, it proved a disaster. Jean Pierre found himself with access to too many accounts from which he could borrow, as he put it. At first he would return the money when he could but I think it all became too easy for him and soon he stopped even trying. I knew something of what was happening and begged him to stop but he would not listen. Then the day that I had warned him about finally came. Quite by chance I discovered from the auditors I deal with that they were to carry out an investigation of his office.

A colleague of Jean Pierre's was worried about irregularities.'

Elinor, who had been listening patiently, could not resist cutting in.

'So that was what the phone call was about?'

'Yes. I told him of the imminent danger and in characteristic fashion he took flight. He faxed in his resignation and broke off all contact with friends and family so that he could not be traced.'

'And what happened to the investigation?'

'As it happened, Jean Pierre had covered his tracks rather well. Nothing was ever proved in his absence and to this day I do not believe Luc is aware of his brother's borrowings. Yet now it seems that Jean Pierre has again acted dishonestly. I know you cannot tell me exactly what he has done but, please, tell me this. If he succeeds, will he harm his brother? Luc has always been good to me, and I would not like to see him suffer.'

Elinor's voice was clear and emphatic.

'If I don't stop him he will ruin his brother's reputation.'

'Then I will help you.'

With one agile movement Marianne was on her feet. Strolling across to a desk placed against the wall she pulled down a leaf, picked up a gold fountain pen and wrote on a piece of writing paper. Elinor, who had followed her, and was looking over her shoulder exclaimed in surprise.

'Texas?'

Marianne straightened and turned to hand the scented, lavender-coloured sheet to Elinor.

'It is where his mother lives.'

'And you're sure he's there?'

'Oh, yes. I gave him the money for the air fare.'

★　★　★

'Texas?' Catriona repeated, like a replay of her friend's reaction earlier.

They were sitting in the car, still parked in the driveway.

'He's staying with his mother,' Elinor explained. 'Apparently he has a habit of going there when he needs to lie low.'

Catriona contemplated her friend's next move.

'You're not really considering going there, are you?'

'I must. It's the only way to retrieve those documents and prove my innocence to Luc.'

'There's no guarantee Jean Pierre will give them to you, especially if he's going to make a mint by selling them. Besides, what if he becomes violent?' she added warningly.

'Jean Pierre may have many weaknesses, Cat, but no-one has ever suggested he might be dangerous!'

'There's your work to consider, too. This is a dream assignment for you and Andrew's already annoyed because you've spent time out chasing after Jean Pierre. What will he say when you tell him you're off to the States?'

Elinor's face clouded.

'He's going to be furious, and he'll probably remove me and assign someone else.'

'But you're still going?'

'Yes.'

With a resigned air Catriona started up the engine and they set off.

'You must really love the guy,' she added.

Elinor, who had never revealed the full depth of her feelings for Luc, let silence answer for her and as they swung out on to the road and headed for Paris, Catriona's next words confirmed her reluctant acceptance of her friend's intentions.

'As your mind is quite set, Ellie, I think we'll go straight to the travel agent when we get back to town. Monsieur Toussant is the best there is. If you want a seat on the next plane to the States he'll ensure you're on it!'

Elinor flashed her a look of gratitude before settling back into her seat.

9

Stepping out from the hotel foyer, Elinor glanced from side to side, made a dash across the pedestrian crossing before the lights had a chance to change, and then rested against the stone parapet of a bridge over the river which snaked its way through the heart of downtown San Antonio but Elinor's mind was not on the colourful scene before her.

Her thoughts were still rooted in Paris and the prickly conversation she had had with Andrew before leaving. There had been no disguising his annoyance at her pre-occupation with her personal problems and she hadn't dared tell him she was coming to the States during the short break she was taking from covering the talks. If she didn't wrap things up as speedily as possible she'd no doubt Andrew would make good his threat to assign another journalist to the assignment.

Luc had given her ten days to return the documents before alerting the authorities and, in spite of missing sleep in order to get here as quickly as possible, it was now seven days since that ultimatum. If she didn't return the documents in time and Luc made a public disclosure it would destroy his reputation and precipitate a crisis at the talks.

A clock on the façade of a hotel which fronted the river walk struck the hour reminding her that her rental car was due to arrive shortly and she had yet to eat. She settled for a nearby Mexican diner which promised authentic cuisine. After her meal, she pulled a road map from her bag, and once more went over the route to her destination which a friendly clerk at the hotel had helped her to work out. She was unaware of the waiter hovering at her elbow until a discreet cough drew her eyes to a friendly smile.

'Senorita, you want some coffee, perhaps?'

'No, but the meal was delicious, thank you.'

Elinor rose to her feet abruptly, unfolded some notes which she left on the table and hurried off. Returning to the hotel lobby Elinor was faced with a smiling receptionist holding up a set of car keys.

'Your rental car is here, Miss Dale. It's in the hotel parking lot and, Ben, here, will take you through.'

She nodded in the direction of the porter, a tall, young man with a mop of curly brown hair who gestured for Elinor to follow. As she did so her spirits began to rise. Soon she would be face to face with her quarry and able at last to ask the questions which had been buzzing inside her head ever since Luc had revealed his brother's treachery.

Forty-five minutes later she was wondering if she would ever run Jean Pierre to ground as she found herself amongst a maze of wide boulevards bordered by gracious houses in Spanish, colonial-style with names which sounded bewilderingly similar to each other. She was busy scanning the names of the houses on the gate posts as she drove past at a sedate pace when the words, Casa Del Rio, woven in gilt lettering into an archway of wrought iron jumped out at her. She drew the large car to a halt, climbed out and then checked the address with the one which was written on the piece of paper given to her by Marianne. It was the same!

Expectation firing her heels she began to walk up the driveway. The heat was stifling but she barely noticed as she made her way to a two-storeyed house painted a brilliant white, the unshuttered windows in dark wood, and the studded door shut firmly against her. She jabbed at the bell to the right of the door and steeled herself for a response as its shrill sound broke the silence. Nothing stirred. Her patience snapping, she rang again and again, only to be greeted by the returning quiet of the afternoon.

Foolishly it had never occurred to her that Jean Pierre could be out. Resting her hands on her hips she stepped back and surveyed the property, noting the path which ran across the front of the house and then wound round to her right. Perhaps she could come across a member of staff who could tell her more. She began to follow the path, and came to an abrupt halt as she found herself in a paved area dominated by a huge kidney-shaped swimming pool. Assorted tables, vividly coloured parasols and loungers were scattered around and one of them was occupied.

Jean Pierre's eyes travelled up Elinor's tall, slim figure and came to rest on the her face, surprise written into his features.

'So, Elinor,' he said, breaking the tense silence, 'it was you disturbing the peace just now.'

'As you see,' she returned acidly, adding. 'Doesn't anyone answer the door around here?'

He gave an elegant shrug.

'It's Maria's day off, and mother's shopping in the local mall, so there isn't anyone to do these little domestic chores.'

His words jarred but she controlled her annoyance, telling herself that he was just set on provoking her. There were other ways to deal with Jean Pierre. She covered the distance between them with a few easy strides before sitting down in a canvas chair. She sat in silence, waiting for him to make the first move, her eyes fixed unwaveringly on him and when she noticed a pulse beating madly at his temple she gave an inner sigh of satisfaction. Jean Pierre was not quite as composed as he was trying to make out. At last he broke the silence with an abrupt question.

'What exactly are you here for, Elinor?'

'Perhaps I just wanted to see you again, Jean Pierre. After all we were very close, once.'

His gaze pulled away and she sensed an inner struggle, conflicting emotions playing out on his features as she waited, content that she had thoroughly unsettled him. He exhaled suddenly and, jumping to his feet, he turned his back on her to pull on a beach robe which had been slung across a table. Whipping round, the words burst out of him.

'Stop this, Elinor, this pretence that you are still interested in me.'

'Why should it be a pretence?' she said mockingly.

'Because I saw the contempt in your eyes when you faced me across the room at the chateau. There was nothing left of the feelings we once shared.'

There was no disguising the sense of injury in his voice and the breathtaking cheek of the man pushed Elinor beyond the bounds of self control. Leaping to her feet she flung her words at him.

'We shared nothing, Jean Pierre, except an illusion, that you could care for anyone but yourself!'

She could see the shock register on his face and his voice, when he spoke, was taut.

'I would appreciate it, Elinor, if you would stop playing games. Say what you have come all this way to say, and then leave.'

'I've come for the documents you stole from Luc's safe. I'm going to return them to him.'

There was silence and Elinor, still facing Jean Pierre's back, was suddenly confronted with the sight of his shoulders heaving. Annoyance stabbed through her. She had come prepared for any number of different reactions from Jean Pierre, from fury to denial, but she had hardly expected amusement! Still chuckling, he turned around to meet her indignant eyes.

'I am sorry, Elinor, but you will never cease to amaze me! Tell me, did you intend to wrestle me to the ground and force me to disclose the whereabouts of the stolen goods or have you got a concealed weapon in that elegant handbag of yours?'

Determined not to be rattled by his ridicule she said, with a control she was far from feeling, 'At least, you are not denying your treachery.'

He opened his arms wide and swung away from her.

'Why not? There is no-one here but you and I.'

He stopped suddenly, suspicion darkening his face.

'Unless, of course, you have the police secreted nearby.'

His eyes darted behind her but her answering flush told him all he needed to know and his face relaxed into a mockery of a smile.

'I see. No one knows that you have come here, do they, not even my self-righteous brother?'

'I haven't come here to talk about myself. I want to know how you intend to repair the damage you've done.'

'I don't. When I get to New York I intend to look up some old friends who will be mighty interested in what I have to show them. This sort of commercial information is worth a fortune, and I'll make darned sure that nothing about this transaction can be traced back to me. I've fooled the authorities once. I can fool them again.'

He was revelling in his dishonesty! How could she ever have deemed this man, ruthless and calculating as he was, to be worthy of her love? Brushing a shaky hand through her hair she closed her eyes for one, brief moment as she fought an internal battle for self control. Right now she had to focus on forcing Jean Pierre to face up to the implications of his actions. She continued, her voice trembling.

'Even if you do not care about the impact your thieving might have on the trade talks, surely you care about Luc's reputation. News of this could destroy him.'

'Good.'

He spat the word out and as Elinor looked at him in dismay, his next words confirmed the depth of his resentment against his brother.

'Ruining Luc's life adds spice to the whole thing, you know. The money will be useful, certainly, but dragging my dear brother down makes the risk all the more worthwhile.'

Elinor felt impelled to ask why he hated his brother so much and was ill prepared for the look of venom which fleeted across his face.

'Because he turned Papa against me! He poisoned his mind with lies about my lifestyle and stole Chateau Pascal, my birthright, from me.'

'Luc is the elder brother. It's only natural he should inherit the estate.'

'Not in France. It is customary to divide the inheritance.'

That was true and Elinor tried another tack.

'You were compensated in kind,' she pointed out.

'With a pathetic trust fund? That hardly pays my wine bill. And whilst I'm scraping around for money, Luc lives in grand style and bars me from the house. Where's the justice in that, Elinor?'

'It's hardly surprising Luc denies you access as you break in and steal from him when he's not there!'

'Just taking what Luc owes me in another form.'

As he stared implacably at her she found herself taking a card with her hotel's name and address on it from her handbag.

'I'm taking a midnight flight out of San Antonia and I'll be at this hotel until then,' she said, handing it over. 'If you do decide to return the documents, call me before I leave.'

'Don't hold your breath.'

Jean Pierre screwed the card up and dropped it at his feet. In that moment Elinor gave up all hope of saving Luc's reputation, and with it their relationship. Jean Pierre had won, but there was still something she needed to know.

'I guess we won't meet again, Jean Pierre. In which case, perhaps you won't mind telling me something?'

'Don't you ever stop asking questions?'

'Only until I get answers. Exactly how did you get into the safe, when I'd torn up the paper with the combination on it before you got there.'

'Why do you want to know?'

'Because Luc thinks I helped you.'

He threw his head back and gave a great bark of laughter.

'So, my brother even got that wrong, did he? Well, you might have torn up the combination but you didn't tear up the pad you'd written it on, did you? I could see that the safe had been opened recently and noticed the indentation on the pad where the numbers had been scribbled. Shading with a pencil brought them up beautifully. It was a simple, childish trick, Ellie!'

She swung away from him, wanting only to get away from his cruel, triumphant smile. As she did so, from the corner of her eye, she caught a glimpse of a diminutive figure standing in the shadows of a ground-floor room. The patio doors were open. She blinked back the tears that were blurring her vision but as she did so the figure seemed to melt away.

10

Elinor glanced down at her watch and realised, with a sinking heart, that it had only been a few minutes since her last time check and she still had an hour to go before the cab arrived to take her to the airport.

Jean Pierre wouldn't come now. She had had little expectation of success as she had fled his home but a tiny part of her had hoped that, after reflection, Jean Pierre might just have a change of heart. She would still insist on thinking that Jean Pierre had a heart! Her mind raced ahead to when she would finally arrive in Paris and have to face the disastrous consequences of her failed mission. She could hardly bear to think about it.

There was a loud knock on the door. Jean Pierre had come after all! She tore across the room, flung open the door, and found herself face to face with a petite, middle-aged woman with gleaming brown hair.

Recognition dawned.

'You're Jean Pierre's mother!'

'Julia del Rio, and you must be Elinor Dale.'

Elinor took the offered hand, saying, 'I recognised you from your portrait at Chateau Pascal. Please, come in.'

Julie complied, her gaze coming to rest on Elinor's face.

'Miss Dale, I realise you will be leaving soon. I will not waste your time.'

Only then did Elinor notice that she was holding a valise in black leather and as her glance fell on to it, Julia set it down on the coffee table.

'This contains all the documents Jean Pierre stole from Chateau Pascal. I can assure you that they have not been copied. Please, Miss Dale, make sure that they are returned safely to Luc.'

Elinor's features lit up with a brilliant smile.

'Thank you so much! You don't know how much this means to me.'

'And to me, too.'

Julia's glance fell, a blush darkening her cheeks and Elinor found herself asking, 'Look, would you like to have a drink with me? I've plenty of time before my flight.'

Julia gave a decisive nod of her head.

'I'd like that. It would be good to talk.'

As they settled themselves down in adjacent chairs with their drinks Elinor turned to the older woman and broke the strained silence.

'You were there at the house, weren't you? You overheard what I said to Jean Pierre?'

A rueful smile crossed her face.

'I thought you might have caught a glimpse of me! I wasn't deliberately eavesdropping, you know. I'd come back from the shops, was on my way outside to let Jean Pierre know, and came across the two of you having the most terrible row. You were so busy

177

yelling at each other you had no idea anyone else was there! I wanted to know what on earth was going on so I shrank back into the shadows and listened. I only caught the end of your argument but it was enough to make me want to know the rest. I made Jean Pierre tell me everything.'

Feeling that a response was called for, Elinor commented, 'You must have been terribly shocked.'

'I was horrified. Finding out that Jean Pierre was a thief was bad enough, but to think that he intended to ruin his elder brother! I knew I had to try and undo the wrong, in order to save both my sons.'

'You must have a good deal of influence with Jean Pierre to be able to force him to co-operate,' Elinor couldn't help pointing out.

'I believe I am the only person alive who does have influence with him.'

She sighed, and Elinor could see the thinly disguised pain in her eyes.

'Much of this mess is my fault, you

know. When I left my first husband I agreed to leave our sons in France. It seemed the right thing to do at the time but the decision proved disastrous for Jean Pierre. He clashed continually with his father and without me there to guide him he began to show all the weakness of character which has led him into dishonesty.'

'And what will happen to Jean Pierre now?' Elinor asked.

'I have persuaded him to stay on with me indefinitely. There is much talking we have to do and much we have to put right, but I hope, in time, that my younger son will learn better ways.'

Elinor hoped so, too. With the indomitable Julia at his side there was at least a chance for Jean Pierre. Julia was now speaking again.

'As for my other son, my proud and principled Luc, please tell him what I have just told you. I don't expect him to be troubled by his brother again. And when you do see him, give him my dearest love.'

'Of course,' Elinor said, her emotions threatening to overwhelm her.

Julia rose and turned away and when Elinor stood up with her, she turned back, as though on impulse, and clasped her hand.

'I know of your past plans to marry Jean Pierre, my dear. You have such courage and spirit I want you to know that I would have loved to have you for a daughter-in-law,' she murmured.

Watching her walk away Elinor wondered what Julia's reaction would be if she were to tell her that that was still her ambition!

* * *

Luc was standing head and shoulders above the small crowd in the arrivals hall and Elinor's heart somersaulted at the sight of him. In a snatched telephone conversation whilst she had been waiting to change planes she had managed to relay the place and time of her arrival but there had been no time for anything else. Although she longed for their re-union and the distance she had to cross was short, her legs felt suddenly leaden and it took all her resolve to walk towards him, her head held high.

Then she was looking up into the face which had haunted her dreams since their bitter rift. She was alarmed by what she saw. Fine lines fanned out from eyes widened and dark, the skin was pulled tautly across his high cheekbones and his mouth was set in a thin, straight line. She felt an almost overwhelming desire to reach up and stroke the lines from his face, to tell him that all was now well and that she had freed herself from the past and was ready to embrace the future.

Instead she handed over the valise with the words, 'This contains all the documents. None has been copied.'

'I know. Jean Pierre called me just before you arrived. He told me you two had decided to cut your losses and return everything. I suppose I should be grateful he had the decency to tell me himself.'

'He's lying! That's not how it is. We were never working together. I went after Jean Pierre to get the documents returned for your sake, for you, Luc! You must believe me!'

'Why should I,' he rapped, 'when everything points to your guilt?'

Her heart constricted as a look of unbearable pain crossed his face.

As though the words were dragged unwillingly from him, he said, 'From the first moment I saw you, Elinor, my life has been turned upside down. For a long time I chased a dream, a hope that we could be together, but the events of the past week have brought me down to earth with a crash and I now accept that I was chasing an impossible dream. So please don't look at me with feigned innocence and tell me I am wrong!'

Through lips numb with shock Elinor made one last attempt.

'If you won't believe me, speak to your mother.'

'Don't bring her into this! She knows nothing of this sordid tangle!'

Elinor almost shrank back from the fury in his face. As though aware that his emotions were running dangerously out of control he made a visible effort to master himself.

'I must go now but I want you to know that I will keep my side of the bargain. Neither you or Jean Pierre will be bothered by the authorities.'

She watched him walk away, dazed at the speed with which her hopes, sky high after Julia's intervention, had now been trampled underfoot because of one last act of spite on Jean Pierre's part.

★ ★ ★

Catriona's face was a picture of indignation.

'You mean the guy just walked out on you, after all you'd done for him?'

'As far as Luc was concerned I'd simply cut my losses rather than face the police. I was a fool, Cat. By letting Jean Pierre know Luc thought I'd helped him, I handed him one last weapon. He might have had to give up the documents but his phone call to his brother just confirmed Luc's suspicions that I was part of the scam.'

'Jean Pierre's mother has a long way to go before she can reform that young man,' Catriona said scathingly, 'but what about Julia? She could speak to Luc for you.'

Elinor's voice was weary.

'Julia and Luc have not had any contact for some time. When I was desperately trying to get Luc to believe me I mentioned her name and it was enough to throw him into a black fury. It's no use, Cat. Luc is determined to believe the worst and I'm too weary to fight for him any more.'

'It's not like you to give up, Ellie,' Catriona said.

'What can I do? Luc has set his heart against me and no amount of reasoning will change his mind. Perhaps this is all for the best. You see, right from the beginning, my involvement with the Pascal family has brought only heartache. The tensions and conflicts that swirl around that family have ensnared me, too, disrupted my life and made me chase after an impossible goal. Luc has let me down badly and I don't think I can ever forgive his loss of trust. I put everything on the line for him, and he chose to believe his lying, cheating brother instead of me.'

There was a bitter truth to her words and Catriona had no immediate response. As the silence lengthened she searched around for something that would prompt her friend out of her gloomy mood.

'At least you'll be starting back at work tomorrow. You'll be too busy to worry about your personal problems, then,' she said finally.

'I'm afraid not. I had a very uncomfortable conversation with Andrew when I got back. He's assigned someone else to the job in Paris.'

'Oh, Ellie.'

Lost for words, Catriona gazed in consternation.

'Anyway, I really need to make some plans. I can't depend on your hospitality for much longer.'

'You can stay as long as you like.'

'No!' Elinor softened her interruption by curving her mouth into a wide smile. 'Look, don't think I'm not grateful for everything you've done. I would have been lost without you, Cat, but it's time to go home. In fact, I think I'll go and give Dad a call right now.'

She bustled out of the room, leaving her friend to stare after her with a worried expression on her face.

* * *

Elinor slotted the last of the chrysanthemums into the vase and placed it on the grave, her fingers automatically tracing the gilded name of her mother cut into the smooth marble of the headstone. Then she scooped up the discarded flowers and straightened. As she walked back towards the church, to dispose of the unwanted blooms, she breathed in deeply and detected a definite nip in the air. Autumn is taking a hold, she thought, and soon the leaves will turn and fall, making way for the icy blasts of winter.

She did not hear a vehicle come to a sudden halt nearby and only became aware of someone else's presence when the sound of a heavy tread swung her round. Dad must have decided to join her after all. A tall figure stooped beneath the lych-gate and, as he straightened, dark brown eyes locked with hers and Elinor felt a shock so acute it was like a physical force.

She had never expected to see Luc again, had persuaded herself that her life was more peaceful without his turbulent presence but now he was only a few feet from her and making no attempt to disguise the love in his eyes. She whipped round, ready to flee.

'No, Elinor, wait!'

With a few strides, he was upon her but as his hand reached out to detain her, she recoiled from him. Pain seared his face.

'What are you doing here?' she hissed. 'I thought I had disrupted your comfortable existence quite enough.'

'I have behaved like a crazy fool, if you'll just listen.'

'Why should I?' Elinor said, fury firing her words. 'You would never listen to me, Luc. You believed me guilty on flimsy evidence and the word of your no-good brother. You broke my heart and a few fine words can't erase all that pain.'

'Ma chère.'

The endearment, as soft as a gentle caress, caused her to close her eyes as she attempted to steel herself against his honeyed words.

'What you say is absolutely true. And when your friend, Catriona — '

'Catriona! What has she got to do with this?'

Luc's lips curved into a rueful smile.

'Everything! You see, I found an angry, young woman on my doorstep one morning. She harangued me for my treatment of you and gave me a list of my faults which began with arrogant and ended with pig-headed. Oh, and along the way she added other insults which, in spite of my mastery of English, were quite new to me!'

In spite of herself, Elinor managed a tremulous smile and Luc, encouraged by this first sign of a thaw, pressed on.

'She told me what had really happened and asked me to confirm it with my mother. That I did, and then I took a cold, hard look at myself. I disliked what I saw. You see, I had never felt certain of your love and when I was tested I allowed my insecurity to poison my judgement. I betrayed the deep love I feel for you and I will never forgive myself for that.'

It was quite an admission for such a proud man to make and Elinor's heart turned over at the sight of the desolate expression on his face. In that heart-stopping moment she knew that they had both suffered enough and she put out one tentative hand.

'Luc,' she whispered tenderly.

★ ★ ★

Next morning he was cradling her face with strong, gentle hands, his dark eyes sending out an unmistakable message.

'Ma chère, we must never be apart again. Say that you will be my wife, that you will be mine for ever.'

'I will,' she breathed.

Much later, perched on a grassy bank overlooking the valley in which the village nestled, they watched the setting sun and discussed their future.

'I'd like your mother to come to our wedding,' Elinor confided. 'I found her to be quite an extraordinary woman.'

To her relief, Luc agreed.

'It's about time the rift was healed. Talking to her recently has already helped to start the healing process and I am so happy now that I want everyone to share our joy. There are other things that need working out, too, such as how to reconcile our two careers.'

Elinor gave a dismissive shrug.

'What career?'

Luc's arm tightened around her as he turned her towards him.

'There is something I must tell you, dear Elinor. You see, I have spoken to Andrew and he has agreed to reinstate you.'

The delight showed in Elinor's face, then she asked, with mock suspicion, 'And how did you achieve this miracle?'

'I was shameful. I told him I was keen to give his newspaper further, exclusive interviews, but only to you. I do hope you are not angry with me for using my influence on your behalf.'

Elinor's laughter rang out.

'I will not be angry with you, my love, as long as you promise to grant me exclusive rights until the end of our days.'

'I agree,' he said, with mock solemnity, one hand placed over his heart.

'And I am a man who loves to fulfil his promises.'

Elinor captured his mouth with her soft lips and drew him into an embrace which signalled a new and hopeful beginning.

THE END

We do hope that you have enjoyed reading this large print book.

Did you know that all of our titles are available for purchase?

We publish a wide range of high quality large print books including:
Romances, Mysteries, Classics
General Fiction
Non Fiction and Westerns

Special interest titles available in large print are:
The Little Oxford Dictionary
Music Book, Song Book
Hymn Book, Service Book

Also available from us courtesy of Oxford University Press:
Young Readers' Dictionary
(large print edition)
Young Readers' Thesaurus
(large print edition)

For further information or a free brochure, please contact us at:
Ulverscroft Large Print Books Ltd.,
The Green, Bradgate Road, Anstey,
Leicester, LE7 7FU, England.
Tel: (00 44) **0116 236 4325**
Fax: (00 44) **0116 234 0205**

THREE TALL TAMARISKS

Christine Briscomb

Joanna Baxter flies from Sydney to run her parents' small farm in the Adelaide Hills while they recover from a road accident. But after crossing swords with Riley Kemp, life is anything but uneventful. Gradually she discovers that Riley's passionate nature and quirky sense of humour are capturing her emotions, but a magical day spent with him on the coast comes to an abrupt end when the elegant Greta intervenes. Did Riley love Greta after all?